Foods, Fools, *and a* Dead Psychic

an Echo Canyon Press publication
Printed in the United States of America

* * *

* * *

Helen Cassidy Page at: Editing Services
http://dailywritingcoach. weebly.com

Cover Design by Mariah Sinclair

Formatting by Debora Lewis
deboraklewis@yahoo.com

ISBN-13: 9798201333812

Foods, Fools, *and a* Dead Psychic

Maria Grazia Swan

Remembering

little no name girl

so loved–so missed

RIP

ONE

Five o'clock and Desert Homes Realty exuded the quietness of day's end. I grabbed the chance to find my boss, Sunny Novak, alone in her office and seek her advice regarding Aunt Brenda. Sunny and Brenda had been close friends for so long I couldn't think of a more qualified person to diagnose my aunt's sudden obsession with food.

I slipped into one of the chairs opposite Sunny's desk and explained, "I blame it on her incident – you know – after the hospital emergency. It's like she traded one obsession for another. She lost her lover but found solace in eating." God, I hated revisiting such a painful event. Even if the overdose was accidental, it had distorted Brenda's personality. Gluttony didn't become someone getting big bucks to tell wealthy, retired folks, how to eat healthy, gourmet meals.

"Life changer." Sunny shook her head, one of her brunette curls falling over her forehead. "Think about it Monica. Twenty years. Gone. Her youth and then some, for that bastard who dropped her without so much as goodbye and then married some Barbie-looking kid half his age."

She slammed the stack of papers on her desk with way too much enthusiasm. Was this hitting close to home? Sunny had just started covering the gray in her lush hair and it couldn't be easy having a sexy twenty-one year old blonde daughter prancing around the office on a show-up-as-you-please basis.

Voices filtered in from the lobby. I hadn't heard the door chime, and apparently neither had Sunny. She frowned then glanced at me. I shrugged, stepped toward the glass wall dividing her private space from the rest of the office area and tried to see who would show up at such a late hour. Whoever it was certainly couldn't expect a tour of available houses for sale. Not after five o'clock and without an appointment. Plus, I was the only licensed realtor still there. My boss worked exclusively with her regular high rollers. The only other soul left in the building was Kassandra who didn't have a real estate license. She took care of the phone, the greetings and other office duties.

Two people stood a few steps outside Sunny's office busily talking to Kassandra. A couple? It was hard to tell because they had their backs to me. Kassandra seemed flustered. Why? Size, spunk and youth were on her side. I quickened my pace.

"Hello," I said, apparently catching them off guard.

The walk-in couple turned at the same time and stared at me like I'd grown a horn on my forehead.

"They're cops, detectives," Kassandra spit out in a hurry as if to get rid of the bad taste the statement left on her lips. "Something happened to Miss Fortune," she added, in a softer tone.

I moved closer to the front lobby. "Miss Fortune? Who's she? A client?" I could feel the detectives' visual assessments volleying between Kassandra and me. And there was nothing playful in the volleying.

"No, not a client. She's — was — the psychic from Tucson? Don't you remember?"

"Oh, yeah, the séance? Yeah I remember. That's when you — uh — lost your…" I stopped. What was I saying? Did I just get Kassandra in trouble?

"She lost what?" the woman cop asked in a forced but sweet tone of voice.

It was my turn to glance from one face to the other.

"It's okay Monica, they know about the bra," Kassandra sighed.

The man stared at me openly and I wasn't sure what to make of that.

"Perhaps we could get a brief report from both of you?" the she-detective suggested with the same sweet-sour voice as before.

"Sure, over a drink? I mean, it's happy hour isn't?" I heard the man chuckle, but the she-cop wasn't amused.

"Coffee and water are free at the precinct." Her tone was not as cut and dried as her hairdo, but close enough. Mercy me.

"Do you know Officer Clarke?" My feeble attempt at clearing the adversarial atmosphere I'd helped create. Clarke was the only local policeman I knew.

"Miss…" She stared at me and waited.

"Oh, Monica, I'm Monica Baker. I'm a realtor here at Desert Homes Realty." I offered my hand. She ignored it.

"Miss Baker, we are detectives, Homicide detectives."

"How exciting…" Fingers crossed, she'd buy my joyful act. "Like Blue Bloods. I just love that show."

Nope, didn't work on her, but her male counterpart fought to keep a straight face. Maybe he liked watching his partner getting all worked up over nothing. Me being the nothing, at least in this case. Was there a connection between Miss Fortune and Kassandra's bra? Returning it to the owner? Poor woman, trying to be helpful and something happened to her? *Something?* These two were h-o-m-i-c-i-d-e cops as in dead, murdered. Poor Miss Fortune. That's when it hit me, Miss Fortune? Say that fast, what do you get? Misfortune... a bad omen for sure.

I hoped Sunny would make an appearance and tell the detectives to leave so she could lock up. What was keeping her?

"This séance? You two went together?" the detective asked.

"No, no." Why did I rush my answer? "I've never done, I mean, been. Never been to a séance. Kassandra told me about it that morning when — you know, she — I — she had no bra and since she's the receptionist." I was babbling and Kassandra didn't seem too happy about it.

"How do you know she wasn't wearing a bra?" The tone of the female detective could freeze an erupting volcano.

How did I know? Seriously? Was she blind? I gave a sideways glance to Kassandra and put my hands up to my flat chest as if gripping a large watermelon. Kassandra rolled her eyes in disbelief, the she-cop shook her head in disgust, and the guy just snickered. Luckily Sunny interrupted my brief miming performance. "What's going on?"

Thirty minutes later, after the detectives collected enough information, or so they said, we locked up the office and headed home.

The instant Sunny's Cadillac left the parking lot, my cell chimed. "Yeah, where to?" I asked.

I followed Kassandra's beat-up Kia to North Italia for their $20 happy hour special. It got a bit complicated because parking at North is strictly valet and the poor kid who rushed over for Kassandra's car couldn't get the Kia to move without a lot of strange engine noises. And the other young man had problems fitting his long legs in my Fiat 500.

But once inside the place, twenty dollars bought us a bottle of their house wine that happened to be an excellent *Pinot Grigio,* and their chef's board to share. We were in a splurging mood and for three dollars more we got to feast on their bowl of paper-thin fried zucchini chips.

We sat on the outside patio. The tall shrubs and potted plants that shielded us from the engine noise of the cars zipping by on 40th Street didn't stop a lingering setting sun from accenting Kassandra's cinnamon colored hair, if only for a nanosecond.

"I'm giving you the short version, and then we'll forget all about it, deal?" Kassandra said.

I shrugged, "It's your bra, your séance. I'm a spectator. And your friend. Go ahead, spill the beans," I said, gingerly stuffing my mouth with crispy zucchini.

"I can't believe the poor woman is dead. I hardly knew her, except for Facebook, but in person? Only met her that evening. Where has she been all this time? She's from Tucson, according to the detectives, her body was found in the canal a week ago, with my bra tied around her neck."

Kassandra stopped to breathe just as our server arrived with the wine. Lucky for us I had my mouth closed when she shared Miss Fortune's — misfortune — or I would have sprayed out my food. Instead, I tried to chew quietly, out of respect for the poor dead woman.

"What else did detectives Adam and Eve tell you?" I fought to wipe the mental image of a dead body floating in a canal wearing someone else's bra around her neck.

"Monica, cops don't tell, they ask. Supposedly it was all over the news because they treated the case as a Jane Doe. Did you hear about it?"

I shook my head no and spread some of that soft cheese on my grilled bread. Apparently the mental image wasn't affecting my appetite. "How can they not know who she was and yet track the bra back to you? Makes no sense."

"You're right. I didn't think about that. There was nothing special about the bra. I usually buy them when they go on sale at Macy's. You buy one at regular price and you get the second half off. I think I've lost my appetite."

She drank her wine and played with one of the olives that were part of the offerings on the chef's board. I don't like olives, something that always makes me the subject of snide remarks because I'm Italian and apparently liking olives should be part of my DNA.

"That's it. Your DNA." I said it a little louder than I meant to, and I could see more than one head turning to stare at our table. Great.

"Get real Monica. The body had been in the water for at least a week according to the detectives. That means my bra soaked in the disgusting canal waters for the same length of time. DNA? Seriously? You watch too many cop shows."

"Hey, just trying to help. So what's next?"

"What's next about what?" Kassandra was still pushing the olives around on her plate. I'm ashamed to confess I ate all the crescenza cheese and had now started my attack on the prosciutto. I shouldn't be enjoying the food, instead I should be sad and depressed like Kassandra. And not knowing the dead woman personally was a poor excuse.

"Wait," I said before biting into a prosciutto-laden bruschetta. "Was she plucked out of a local canal? Like *our* canal? The one running about thirty feet from the back of this restaurant?" And suddenly I did feel awful, probably for the wrong reasons.

"Ah. Now that you mention it... it's possible. I'm not sure if it's the same canal. How many canals are there in Phoenix?"

I shrugged, had no clue. Besides, we weren't talking Venice's Grand Canal. In Phoenix they all looked alike to me.

"You know what? I bet that's why we decided on North Italia... it's that thing, you know, mind association? The body in the canal and the restaurant by the canal. Ewwww. I've also lost my appetite," I said while scooping up the last of the prosciutto. My grandma must be turning in her grave. I had become totally jaded. Blamed it on all the cop shows I watched.

"Let's change the subject." Kassandra sipped more wine, "I need a car, and so do you. You can't seriously expect to drive prospects around in your hot pink Fiat, right?"

Blood rushed to my cheeks. I took criticism of my beloved car very personally. "It hasn't hurt me yet," I declared.

"Come on, Monica. Who do you think you're fooling? So far you've been able to meet clients at the properties. Your luck will run out sooner or later..."

I knew she was right. "I'm waiting until we close on the Tucson horse ranch." Carefully avoiding *his* name.

"Oh, that's right. You'll get a big fat check when Tristan Dumont's escrow closes."

Noooo. She mentioned *his* name. Let the heartache begin.

TWO

December brought shorter days. By seven o'clock sunset was history. Driving east on Camelback Road on my way home, I had to cross over the canal. It felt creepy, even without knowing if this was the canal where Miss Fortune's body had been found. Creepy or not, I planned on Googling the ghoulish story the minute I got home. Between the dead psychic and the mentioning of Tristan Dumont, that flurry at the pit of my stomach wasn't food-related, that was for sure. Another ironic reminder that even going to happy hour with a good friend doesn't guarantee happy anything.

As for Tristan, or to be fair, my obsession with Tristan, I had lulled myself into believing I had built immunity to his charm. This was in theory, of course, because we hadn't spoken since I visited him back at the beginning of November while he was bedridden due to our car accident.

One of his friends drove him to the office after that visit. Tristan moved slowly, walking with a cane. I waved at him, from a safe distance, and then left the real estate office with some lame excuse. Kassandra winked as I walked out the door. Was I so transparent? When I drove out of the parking lot, I had the feeling someone was watching me. Could it be him? From the office window? Why? He was a married man. Nothing good could happen between us… except the obstinate crush I fought hard to keep in check.

I thought of Tristan as a sinful temptation, a residual from my Catholic upbringing, I guess. And I couldn't help comparing that temptation with poor Max every time he came near me. Sheesh, like comparing French bubbly to soda water.

Max — fingers crossed he wouldn't show up at my place tonight. Between Miss Fortune and Tristan… well, the only thing I looked forward to this evening was getting into my pajamas and watching television while searching for details of the mysterious drowning of the psychic. Drowning? There I was, assuming again. Who would tie a bra around the neck of a drowning woman? And why? So she wouldn't catch cold? Stop it, Monica, that's very disrespectful.

But that brought a lot more questions to the surface. Was Miss Fortune naked or did she end up in the canal with her clothes on? I could spin scenarios in my mind all night and still find no logical explanation regarding the bra.

My friend Kassandra's bra.

She hadn't said much to the detectives about why she left it behind at a stranger's house, the same house she had gone to for the séance. There had to be some connection, however, it had been what? Seven weeks since that day? It happened before Tristan's house warming and the house warming was before Thanksgiving. Now here we were, early December although every inch of town was already decked out as if Christmas was but a stroke of the clock away.

I liked to drive home through Paradise Valley even with the forty miles per hour speed limit strictly enforced. Rumor had it that the income from the speeding tickets kept the town of Paradise Valley solvent. That counted for a lot of tickets.

Oh, such a pleasant drive on Tatum Boulevard, unfurling through most of the town, from North to South, from Camelback Mountain to Phoenix Mountain Preserve. Large homes set away from the road, on vast acreage, no horses in sight, and few night lights. The first impression felt a little pastoral. Pastoral? The most expensive dirt in Maricopa County? Okay, Monica, maybe you need to cut down on the Pinot Grigio, especially if it's served by the bottle. In spite of all the promises and good intentions, I made a small detour and drove by Tristan's street. Thanks to the house setbacks and the early darkness, I figured even my hot pink Fiat could zip by unnoticed... while my heart bounced up and down in my chest like butter on a hot griddle.

Five minutes later I turned into our street.

Brenda's porch light was on. She must be home. I didn't see any car parked up front. Good. I drove to the back and into my garage. No sign of Max's truck or Tommy's motorcycle. With the coast clear, my mood improved and I knocked on Brenda's back door. Dior barked me in.

"Okay, okay, down boy, I know you love me, I love you too." The Great Dane acted like he hadn't seen me in a million years.

"Does he need to go potty?" I asked Brenda who sat on her usual spot on the couch, a glass of wine in her hand, a pack of smokes on the coffee table next to an empty bag of potato chips, same brand she often reminded me not to eat. Brenda Baker, my ex-husband Tommy's aunt and the only family I had this side of the ocean.

Just as nice and loving as before her hospital detour, except now she took up more space on the couch and her clothes looked like they had been run through the wrong dryer cycle. A couple of times I suggested she should get some new threads, at least for work. Brenda would look at me, without a word, a blank stare in her eyes, a reflection of the emptiness inside?

"Dior? No, he's good. You hungry?" I noticed her television was on. The sound barely audible. Would she ever be the old Brenda she was before the accidental overdose?

"I stopped for happy hour with Kassandra. What are you watching?" I scratched the dog's ears to keep him off me.

"Not sure, there isn't much on," she clicked from channel to channel, distracted by whatever her mind tackled between her long silences and her brief bursts of life.

"Wait, wait, what's that? Go back," I squealed.

She did, and turned to look at me, "What? That?" She pointed her TV control to the screen where the sketch of an older woman's face stared back at us. "That's the Jane Doe they fished out of the canal and..."

"The canal?" I babbled. "Miss Fortune." It had to be her.

"I guess it is indeed, a misfortune for the poor woman and..."

"No, I mean her name is Miss Fortune, at least that's what Kassandra said."

"Kassandra – your office Kassandra? She knew the poor woman?"

"Please stop calling her poor woman, she is – was – a psychic, from Tucson."

Brenda rested the wine glass on the coffee table and turned to stare at me. "The name sounds familiar – Miss Fortune." She repeated slowly. "And you think she's a psychic? You need to tell the authorities. They are showing the artist rendering hoping someone would recognize her. Maybe she came to town for the fair."

"The fair? What fair? The cops already know. They came to the office and questioned Kassandra. Because of the bra."

"Monica, how much happy do you drink at these happy hours?"

I should have been insulted but wasn't, because for the first time in a long, long while Brenda's eyes didn't look like bottomless dark holes. They looked human.

"It's true. I can't figure out how they tracked Kassandra through a bra. It's not DNA, at least Kassandra doesn't think so, because she said the body was in the canal for a week?"

"Bra? Custom made maybe?"

"I asked, she said she buys them at Macy's when they are on sale."

"So, this — Miss Fortune — she knew Kassandra because of the Tarot cards? Or did they meet at the Psychic Fair?"

I blinked. "What's with this Psychic Fair? Where is it? How do you know about it? I assumed the detectives questioned Kassandra because of the séance."

"What séance?" She really perked up. I had no idea Brenda was interested in that kind of stuff. Anyway, this was getting complicated and boring. I couldn't wait to go back to my place, the guesthouse in the back, and do my own investigating with the help of Google.

"A bunch of people got together and hired Miss Fortune to do a séance where you communicate with — the spirits?" I forgot. "Anyway, a few weeks ago the psychic came up from Tucson, by bus. Kassandra was to drop her off at the bus station the next morning, on her way to work. She spent the night in the home where the séance took place, but the man who owns the house tried to — you know—" I hesitated, my old Catholic up-bring kicking into high gear.

"Know what?"

"He tried to — have sex with Kassandra. So she grabbed her stuff and ran out of the house and drove away. She left her bra and Miss Fortune behind."

"Oh. And you think the woman came back to town for the fair and decided to return the bra to the rightful owner?"

"After all this time?" I felt compelled to add. "It all happened before the Dumont's housewarming party that we catered. Besides, I don't know who found the bra Kassandra left behind. And I don't remember Kassandra ever mentioning a local fair. How do you know about it?"

Brenda sipped her wine. "I read about it in the paper. I'm pretty sure they have events like that often, in large hotels, you know. Don't take my word for it, you can probably find out on the Internet. It may even show the list of the psychics, astrologers, mediums who participated and probably the tarot readers."

On the screen the reporter was interviewing an older man with a fishing pole. Must be the lucky soul who hooked the corpse. "I'm confused, how come I don't know any of that stuff? It sounds sort of interesting. Do they tell you the future? Oh, I get it. You're saying the psychic from Tucson was in town for the fair. When was it again?"

A car door slammed somewhere outside. Yikes! Were my pajama and TV plans about to be snuffed out? Soon followed a soft knock on Brenda's front door. I looked at her, stretching her legs and pushing the pack of cigarettes and empty chips bag under a stack of magazines. Ah! "Officer Clarke?" I asked, sporting my best Cheshire smile.

"His first name is Robert." She rolled her eyes, ran her fingers through her hair. She walked toward the door, brushing off a few dry crumbs from the front of her blouse, Dior at her heels. While I headed to the back door I heard her say to me, "Bob to his friends."

I hurried to let myself out through the back door before Bob made his entrance.

NONE OF THE snippets I found on the Internet identified Jane Doe as Miss Fortune. At least not yet. What if that wasn't her real name? I mean, how perfect was that combination? Your local psychic, Miss Fortune. I googled the name. Fortune didn't bring up anything related to a drowning victim, but a lot of stuff about Fortune 500 and business magazines. I tried Miss Fortune and for a minute I thought I'd hit the jackpot. Well, on closer look, I hadn't. The Facebook page with that name belonged to a now gone musician or band. It also appeared to be the name of some mythical legendary fighter. Disappointed, I turned off the computer and went to bed. I had three voice mail messages from Max. If I didn't listen to them I wouldn't feel obliged to reply. I wasn't proud of myself, not a bit but didn't know how to get out of the situation without feeling even guiltier for breaking Max's heart, again.

That night I dreamed of Tristan, like the night before and the night before that.

THREE

"Must buy a car, must buy a car," I repeated over and over in my mind, like a mantra, hoping it would do the trick. No need to sell or trade my Fiat. Against all logic, I had come to consider the pink car my lucky charm. It had been a gift from my father-in-law, Brenda's brother. To him, it didn't matter I was already divorcing Tommy, or maybe it did matter and it was his way of letting me know it was all right. Married to Tommy or not, I'll always be a member of the Baker family. That was a big part of my attachment to the car and the easiest to explain. I grew even more attached once Tristan Dumont nicknamed me Fiat. The rest had to do with vague feelings of patriotic pride, Fiat being an Italian brand and all that.

Brenda had suggested a four-door sedan, slightly used, with low mileage so it would still be under warranty. The idea sounded practical, if not exciting. I could use my share of the commission from the horse ranch and finance the rest if necessary. I didn't have a set dollar figure because the Dumont's ranch deal happened while I was still employed as Sunny's assistant and had no legal claim to a commission. Regardless, she offered to share with me. Escrow closing had been dragging due to unpaid taxes and the seller's attempt at skirting responsibility. Lawyers from both sides were busy sorting everything out. I avoided the subject as much as possible. Somehow, associating Tristan with my paycheck felt too... mercenary.

The next morning I proudly crossed the threshold of Desert Homes Realty before nine a.m. A first. But instead of Kassandra's familiar face, who sat on her chair but Scott, our signs installer and all around handyman. Weird.

Phones rang. Scott didn't seem in a hurry to answer them. I could see real estate agents in the back, the so-called bullpen, none paying much attention to the front lobby turmoil. "Where is Kassandra?" I asked.

Scott shrugged, "Home?" Had all twenty-somethings taken a vow to speak in the fewest words possible or was it just tall, muscular sign installers?

"Oh, is she sick?" I asked. I remembered her not eating and only drinking wine at North happy hour last night. Nah, it couldn't be that. I'd seen her guzzle a lot more alcohol and drive home without noticeable side effects.

Scott shrugged. "Sick of the cops maybe. They are at her place, with a search warrant."

"Noooo. Because of the bra?"

"The what?" Finally something sparked his interest and his youthful face lit up. Still he wasn't answering the phones. Lucky for him our boss hadn't arrived yet. Suddenly he got up and grabbed his clipboard. "You need to mind the phones until Kassandra gets here," he said. I've got a schedule to keep."

And before I could compute the meaning of that, his tall frame was out the door. I had no clue how the thing with the flashing buttons worked. All I could do was pick up the phone and answer one call at a time. That alone would be an improvement from what Scott did, or didn't do. And so I answered the calls and made notes instead of forwarding them to the correct extensions. Besides, I had no time to check who was in the back and who wasn't. Some coffee would help, but no one came to my rescue. I sighed and diligently made notes as the calls kept coming. After about twenty-five minutes it all quieted down. Good.

Search warrant. That's what Scott had said. What were the police looking for? I wasn't even sure where Kassandra lived. She'd recently rented a condo in a multi-story complex around Seventh Avenue and Northern, but we never really got into details. I hardly ventured west of Central. Maybe I should call her. What if the cops were still there? All because of a stupid bra. *And a dead psychic*. Better clear my mind and take care of my own business. Someone else could mind the phones. Where was Sunny? Ah, coming through the door at that very moment — with Tristan Dumont in tow. Mercy. He looked so good and no more walking cane. I opened my mouth a few times but no sound made it through. He winked at me.

"Good morning, Fiat."

Three short words, enough to fling the blushing gates wide open.

That must have gotten Sunny's attention because she faced me and frowned, "Where is Kassandra?"

"Huh?"

I had to remember to close my mouth. I must have looked like an idiot, a red faced idiot. "She's home, I guess. Scott was here and... then he left. I've been answering the phones. I'm not very good at it and..."

Under Tristan's amber-eyed scrutiny I could hardly breathe like a normal human being, let alone talk. Something in my dazed behavior must have reached Sunny's consciousness; her attitude changed.

"Monica, I'm so sorry. Thank you for pitching in. Had no idea about Kassandra's absence. Let me see who I can get to cover for her."

Before I could sigh in relief, the front door opened again and Sunny's daughter and reluctant part-time receptionist, Celine, made her grand entrance. She headed straight for Tristan, sashaying to the beat of her stiletto heels and sporting a smile that said, "I only have eyes for you."

Until her mother stepped in front of her.

"Celine," Sunny said. "Perfect timing, I need you to mind the phones while I find out what's going on with Kassandra." I could swear I heard a faint skidding of heels against the tile floors, but maybe it was my lack of caffeine or the excess of lust in the air that played mind tricks on me.

"The phones? Me? But mom, why? Have her do it." She pointed her perfectly manicured finger at me. I didn't even bother to wait for Sunny's response, I headed to my own cubicle, walking stiff like a marionette, painfully aware of Tristan's gaze on me. And what was Celine doing there? You'd think she had Tristan microchipped the way she bulldogged him. To his credit, he barely nodded hello in her direction. His hair had grown; now it was almost the same length as the first time we met. When I had mistaken him for a construction worker three months ago, and yet it felt like a lifetime away. I dropped my things in the limited space I called my own and walked around from cubicle to cubicle to hand out the phone messages I had jotted down on sticky notes. By the responses you'd think these people had forgotten about paper and pen... but some of them reacted rather funnily. One of the post-its happened to be pink and the male agent who got it made a big production of announcing loudly; "It's a girl, it's a girl." Followed by a round of laughter.

I was dying to get myself some coffee, but that meant walking by the front lobby where Sunny and Celine were still locking horns from the sound of it. Where was Tristan?

Oh, no. He had found his way to my cubicle. I spotted him before he turned and smiled.

"There you are." He handed me a business card. "He should be calling you any day now."

I glanced at the card, a fancy law firm and a name followed by Esq. Impressive of course. "What is this for?"

"It's the law firm sorting out the damages and settlement pertaining to our accident." Still holding the card, fingers lingering, so close to mine.

Our accident. We shared something. Was I smiling? Mercy. A true fool. That's what Tristan's presence did to my common sense. I managed a heartfelt, "Oh," just as Sunny caught up to us and called out, "Tristan, Title is on the phone." And with a light nod and a smile, he let go of the business card and followed my boss to her sanctum sanctorum.

My hands trembled. Get a grip Monica, you came to the office to work not to turn to mush because of... enough. I straightened up and marched to the kitchen to get myself some well-deserved coffee. My cell chimed in my pocket as I poured the steaming liquid salvation into my mug. I eyed some leftover bagels. Perfect. Grabbed one, rested it next to the coffee and saw a welcome name on the screen. "Morning, Kassandra."

"Hi, I'm parked across the street, I'm so embarrassed. What did Sunny say?"

"About what? And why are you whispering? I'm in the kitchen, getting coffee and scraping up leftover bagels."

"Is Scott covering for me?"

"Scott left. Look, no one needs to know about the cops and the search warrant."

"You do."

"Scott told me before he disappeared and left me in charge of answering the phones. I haven't told a soul."

"Oh, thank you, thank you. I owe you one. Wait, if you're in the kitchen who is at the front desk?"

"Celine." Long pause.

"Crap. Celine? What the hell is she doing there so early? Wait. I know. I bet the Dumont stud is there." She sighed. "I'm coming in, don't want that spoiled brat to mess up everyone's day. And you're sure? No one knows about, you know... Save me some bagel crumbs. I'm starving." She was gone before I had a chance to slip in a single question about the search warrant. What were the cops looking for? The panties matching the bra?

Being the only one in the kitchen felt liberating. Why would I think that? I lived alone. Well, most of the time, as Brenda and I shared the same driveway. Plus, I had my own cubicle here at the office Maybe it was because the kitchen was like Switzerland... neutral. We all walked through it and tried to leave it as we found it... and... we didn't borrow other people's stuff.

I heard the chime of the front door opening, followed by Celine barking, "About time you made it to work. Next time you decide to sleep in, hire your own substitute."

Immediately followed by a furry of heels clapping on tile. I counted to ten before sticking my head out of the kitchen doorway.

"And a good morning to you, also," I chimed when Her Lateness stumbled past. "Relax. I'll bring your coffee and let you catch up, but we must do lunch because I'm dying to hear about the — c o p s — okay?"

Kassandra gave me a side-glance, shook her head, but I think it was because of her desk's state of disarray. I quickly retreated into the neutral zone and located Kassandra's *Another Day in Paradise* mug. I filled it to the brim with coffee, managed to put together some large pieces of broken bagels, then carried it all to her desk. She looked rested and not sick, at least not in obvious ways.

"Guess what?" she said.

Talk about multitasking. She sipped coffee, munched on stale bagels, redirected phone calls and still tried to maintain a conversation. Wow!

"I think I know how the cops found out it was my bra."

"You serious? How?"

"Crap, one pissed-off blonde heading this way."

I heard the clapping of heels before I saw Celine. Made a quick turn around and went back into my Switzerland-safe-zone. Celine must have not received the note about kitchen neutrality. She flew in, minus the broom, and demanded a clean mug.

"For Tristan," she added with a smug smile. I pointed to the stash on the counter and exited as fast as I could. I barely made it back to my cubicle when I heard a commotion, a crash and an ear piercing shriek. Celine had accidentally dropped the coffee. I peeked at the scene, along with every other agent in the bullpen. The blonde was so angry, she kicked the broken pieces of china around and hissed crazy stuff like "magic potion, what now- no fair." No one moved, knowing her nature. She would have probably retaliated against anyone brave enough to volunteer to help her clean up the mess.

Celine's mother and Tristan Dumont, however, did come out of the glass box to check on the ruckus. The blonde's expression changed and she threw herself against the object of her — affection — landing on his chest in spite of the cool Mr. Dumont showing signs of clear panic while fending off the body-to-body warfare. The whole scene was so comical I didn't even feel a bit jealous, just a whole lot of sadness for all of us involved, willingly or not.

FOUR

By the time I parked my Fiat in the office parking lot, it was past one o'clock and my stomach gurgled loudly. I had bypassed two of my favorite fast food places in order to do lunch with Kassandra, I didn't care where. Today the main item on my menu was pure gossip. Before getting out of the car I scouted the surroundings, checking for familiar cars I wished to avoid. Okay, not the cars, the drivers. Celine's blue Sebring convertible, gone. Sunny's Cadillac, nope, not there. Tristan Dumont's white Land Rover. Get a grip Monica, the Land Rover? Smashed to smithereens when a semi fell on it with you two in it... remember? I had no idea what kind of car he drove now. Better yet, I didn't even know if he was driving. Deep breath Monica and march right in there. I did. Kassandra gave me an exaggerated hand wave and kept talking on the phone. I nodded, walked directly to my cubicle where I dropped my briefcase and proceeded to look for Kay.

Kay was one of the senior agents and had her own little private office. She had also mentored me since the first day I received my license. All that with Sunny's blessing, of course. I wanted to discuss with Kay this new referral I received thanks to Brenda's connections. The couple selling the patio home had already purchased in the Scottsdale retirement resort where Brenda worked as a Registered Dietitian Nutritionist. They took their time, aware it would be their last move, I imagine. Every object, down to the furniture, artwork and rugs had to be itemized. Keep or dump? The shedding now complete, it was time to list their place for sale. This property was in a very nice neighborhood, but the home needed updating. Also, it was in a community that was age restricted, 55 or older. I had no doubt Kay would know exactly how I should handle it.

"Normally I would suggest waiting until after the new year to list. People aren't looking to buy weeks before Christmas," she said. "But with the age restriction factored in and the fact that it would be the only active listing in such a sought-after area, I say go for it. Snowbirds will be flocking in fleeing the harsh winter back East. They may come to visit relatives and who knows? Decide to stay. You need to stage a little, get great pics, some twilight scenes, and since there is a man-made lake on the spot, make sure it gets included in at least a few photos. Create a sense of romance. Never too old for that. Do you know who to hire for the photo shoot?"

I nodded, "Yes, I've been using all the people you recommended from day one. I'm very happy with them. Is it okay if I show you some comps and some of the numbers I'm coming up with? No, not this instant. I've only been inside the home once. Maybe after I meet the photographer. That usually gives me a chance to see every angle, every nook through the fresh eye of a professional."

Kay nodded her head, obviously pleased and I was happy about that. I headed back to my cubicle where I kept my info but before I turned the corner Kay called out to me, "Hey Monica, I hear Colter Cadillac is having a very nice clearance sale."

Ouch. I didn't turn around, didn't stop walking. I raised my hand above my head and waved to let her know I heard her. I listened to her amused laugh chasing me as I walked away. Cadillac, right! Who did she think I was? Tristan Dumont? Back in my cubicle, I looked at everything that sold in my client's neighborhood in the last four months. It wasn't much and everything moved fast. Good. The new year was shaping up to be good as far as real estate was concerned. With the Dumont's horse ranch scheduled to close, and one of my own escrows, a small house I found for a young couple I met at the Doggie Day Care where we took Dior once in a while, and now this property in toney Scottsdale. Good. Kay had mentioned snowbirds visiting for Christmas and suddenly images arose of the Dolomites and Fongara, the mountains close to home where we used to ski as kids... my sister said it had snowed. Stop it, Monica. You can't go home again. Focus.

My cell chimed. "Kassandra? What's keeping you? Are we doing lunch? I'm starving."

"It's complicated," Kassandra replied.

Huh?

"I'm feeling guilty about this morning and Sunny has been more than accommodating. I can't leave the office."

I started to protest.

"Shssh — let me finish. I called Safeway and ordered two pounds of chicken tenders, a pound of kale salad, rolls, butter, the works. Get in your car and park in their pick up slot. They'll bring you the food. It's all paid for. We'll eat in the kitchen. I think there are only four of us left at the office," she continued.

I had to catch my breath; part of me was pissed off she did all that food ordering without even consulting with me. The other part felt pretty good. I liked the Safeway chicken tenders and if Kassandra was right, we'd be eating and gossiping in about eighteen minutes.

"What happened? Cat got your tongue?" Kassandra again. I stood and stepped to the side. I could see her sitting at her desk, looking at me and laughing.

"Where is everyone now that you mention it?" I spoke while getting my purse.

"Double Wide." She said. Ouch. Double Wide was the nickname we had for a new and very aggressive broker who swept into town two months ago, opened a brand new real estate office in a swanky glass and steel building, a rather unusual move in the conservative Arcadia neighborhood. And D.W., the initials of his name, kept doing elaborate open houses intended for poaching the top producers from other real estate offices. Word in our office was he had been courting Kay. Our Kay. So we called him Double Wide even if he really wasn't. I only met him once. I thought he wore very nice Italian loafers and silk ties. And apparently his open houses were always catered. I made a note to ask Brenda what she knew about that.

Twenty minutes later Kassandra and I were slouching in the kitchen. She kicked off her shoes as we chomped furiously through our golden, crunchy chicken tenders.

"From now until January this place will be as quiet as a library," she said.

"Never mind that, I want to hear about the search warrant. What is it the detectives are looking for? Did they mess up your house? What?"

"Monica, you watch too many cop shows. It isn't like that in real life." She scooped a generous helping of kale.

"Maybe, but I know you're avoiding my question. Did you meet Miss Fortune at the Psychic Fair?"

Kassandra stopped, plastic fork in mid air, "You know about the fair?"

"Brenda told me."

"Your aunt went to the fair? I never pictured her as a..."

"Noooo. She read about it in the paper and told me when they were showing Miss Fortune in the news. Stop playing stupid. Did you or did you not go to the fair and run into the poor, you know..."

Kassandra scowled, fiddled with her fork, just as she was doing the other day at North. "I hate this."

"You hate your food?" *She* ordered it.

"No, not the food." She stood and walked barefoot to the kitchen door, then stepped into the small hall and seemed to look around as if checking for someone listening. When she came back and spoke she didn't sound like Kassandra at all, her voice low and her eyes restless. “You can’t repeat this to anyone, you hear me?”

I nodded. What else was I going to do?

“I had signed up for Miss Fortune’s séance and also for a tarot cards class. Both were on Saturday afternoon. I drove there early because I figured I’d get myself some lunch at the sports bar at the hotel. That’s where everything happens and this being the Christmas Fair, there were some big names. Now, while most of the mediums, astrologers and psychics are women, the big names, the big money attention getters, are usually men. They travel the circuit between Vegas gigs. One of the top Energy Therapists in the nation was in town, and I wanted to meet him without paying the big bucks. That’s why I went to the bar.”

“I don’t know what an Energy Therapist is. Anyway, did you meet him?”

“Energy Therapists work to rebalance your energy. That’s the short version. They usually have a medical background and they work with people, mostly women, who have emotional problems like insomnia, overeating, hormonal issues, and no, I didn’t meet him. I did however run into an old friend.” She rubbed her hands as if cleansing them, “I could sure use a drink.”

“You know we aren’t allowed to drink at the office. So who was the old friend? Miss Fortune?” A phone rang once, twice, it must have gone to voice mail.

She shook her head. “A ghost from the past.” She smiled. “A man.” Must have been a pleasant ghost.

"We drank and chatted. He's a rep for a sports equipment manufacturer. He calls the East Coast home. Married with kids. Meanwhile, the séance I signed up for was over and done and I never showed up for my tarot card class. We couldn't go to his room with all the cameras and the people who might know him, so we ended up at my place. He left early in the morning to go back to the hotel and make his flight. The end. Or so I thought. The other evening when the detectives came over to talk to me, they stopped by my condo first. One of the astrologers had recognized the drowned woman from the newspaper sketch and called the police. Apparently Miss Fortune was upset I wasn't at her séance and had been asking if anyone saw me. And, truth be told, there was a message or two from her on my voice mail, but I didn't check my phone until after my friend left. By then it didn't matter. She was looking for a place to crash that night. Of course I feel like crap thinking maybe she would be alive if I had offered her shelter."

I'm ashamed to confess that my first reaction was, see what happens when you sleep with a married man? And the amber eyes of Tristan Dumont winked in my mind's eye.

"After talking to my neighbor, the detectives came to the office, well you know the rest."

"Poor Miss Fortune, maybe she wanted to return your bra."

Kassandra patted me on the knee. "Okay, complete truth, I was the one who told the detective about the bra. Wait, let me finish. They came in with one of the pamphlets from the fair, the one with the pics and bio of all the presenters. They also had a pic of the... you know, her... after they fished her from the water. I don't know if it was planned or purely coincidental but they also had a photo of the bra. Stupid me, thinking I was being funny, said, 'Oh, look at that, you came all the way here to return my bra?' You can fill in the blanks. They didn't take my word regarding Miss Fortune. They came to see if they could somehow place her at my condo the night she went missing. Fat chance. I told them to look at the cameras in the complex, and they'd see who I dragged home with me."

She put her shoes back on, got up and started to clean up our paper plates. I was stunned.

"Aren't you going to finish eating?" Kassandra asked.

I shook my head. Whoa. I just gobbled up a lifetime's worth of bad karma... and I knew that in spite of Kassandra's 'I'm a badass' attitude, she felt terribly guilty. I went to hug her; it felt awkward, her being that tall and busty and all. Christmas was just around the corner and we were both as lonely as could be. I could read it in her eyes.

"I've got an idea," I said. "Tomorrow is Saturday. Can you come over to the house? I need to take the pictures for Christmas cards to send to Italy. Bring your bathing suit."

"What? Bathing suit? It's December. You nuts?"

"It's 75 degrees out. It will melt the ice cubes in our drinks. I do this every December. I send photos of myself, lounging by the pool, drinking tall, colorful drinks with little umbrellas to make my family jealous, hoping they'll decide to come and visit."

"You're a real Italian fruitcake, you know that? What time should I come over?"

FIVE

"Do they have witches?"

Kassandra reapplied her bright red lipstick, and examined the straw hat I had handed to her. "Witches? What are you talking about?"

"You know, the people at the fair? The ones who tell the future."

She shook her head, and the hat slid right off her shiny, cinnamon mane. "I don't know where you get your information but psychics and witches have nothing in common. Aren't you going to change?"

"I think I better go get Dior first." I picked up the reindeer antlers headband I bought on sale at Walgreens. "What do you think? Cute?"

"You are putting that on the Great Dane? And he's letting you?"

"I bribe him." I shook the bag of organic jerky treats for dogs. "Needs to be done before Brenda gets back. He gets very rambunctious when she's around, you know, like a teenager."

"Is he going to jump in the pool? And splash us?"

"Kassandra, relax. Danes are afraid of water. Plus I've done this before. Let me grab the drinks and get this done. Brenda should be back soon; she promised us brunch." I pulled the two plastic flutes with the tiny paper umbrellas from the refrigerator.

"What's that? Wine?" Kassandra didn't seem too convinced.

"It's jelly."

"Huh? Jelly? Fake drinks?"

"That's the only way I could figure out how to get the umbrellas to stay put." We walked to the pool, fake drinks in hand and Dior's antlers and my Santa's hat in a plastic bag. All Kassandra did was shake her head. I left her staring at the pool while I ran over to Brenda's place to get Dior.

"We'll need to take turns with the photos." I explained. "I'll take yours first, you and Dior on the lounge chairs, then I'll trade with you." I removed my shirt to show my bikini so Kassandra didn't feel naked.

"Wait, wait," she said, shocked. "Is that? You have a pierced navel?"

Kassandra sounded like she'd seen a monster popping out of my belly button. I instinctively covered the small zirconia with my hand. "It's old. Happened when I first came to America. My first au pair job was in LA and everybody was doing it, the piercing I mean. I wanted to fit in."

"Well, you'll fit right in with the Energy Therapists. They believe that *piercing* the *belly button* aligns or improves function of the third chakra."

"The third what?"

She laughed and shook her head fighting off Dior who slobbered over her arms, his way of showing interest. I pulled out my phone, pitched Dior a treat. He leaped for it and voilà, I had a terrific photo.

"Look." I passed the phone to Kassandra.

"Hey, pretty neat. Your relatives will think we've been frolicking around all day. Are you going to Photoshop our suntan?" she teased.

I shrugged, moved the jelly-umbrellas drinks to the side and plopped myself on the chair next to her. "Okay, your turn, hey, Dior, stay away from the gate."

Too late, he must have heard Brenda's engine seconds before I did and was pushing up the lock with his nose like he had multiple times before. He took off galloping down the driveway, the antlers now hanging around his massive neck like a discarded Christmas wreath. I had to catch him before he hit the street or was run over by Brenda's Honda Pilot. I lost one of my flip-flops but kept on running.

I could hear Kassandra calling as I rounded the corner and stopped. Brenda's vehicle was parked length-wise in front of our shared driveway, which was a good way of blocking Dior I guess. No sight of Brenda but another SUV, black and spiffy, was parked right behind the Honda. I didn't see anyone, but heard voices, Brenda talking to Dior.

"What happened to you boy? Okay, okay, I love you too. How did you get out? Wait, what's around your neck?"

I knew I only had two options. One, circle the Honda, and explain to Brenda about my harmless Christmas card project — and ask for forgiveness. Or, two, turn around and run back to my place as fast as I could and pretend I knew nothing about anything.

I checked behind me to see what Kassandra was doing. No one there but my lonely flip flop waiting to be rescued. My so-called friend was probably already in my bathroom getting dressed and rehearsing the innocent expression to use while telling Brenda how I tricked her into putting antlers on Dior. While I weighed my options, Brenda appeared, holding Dior's collar since I hadn't put a leash on him, followed close by... nooooo... Tristan Dumont.

Tristan Dumont! What was he doing here? They both stopped dead, sporting the strangest facial expressions I had ever seen. Dior seized the moment of confusion to get away from Brenda, launching himself onto me with all his enthusiasm and weight. The gazillion pound Great Dane knocked me down, with my nearly bare butt going down for a hard landing on the concrete driveway. That pain in my rear end was nothing compared to the humiliation of having Tristan see me splayed out in my half-naked glory.

I opened and closed my mouth a few times as the object of my hopeless desires walked over and extended his hand to help me up. Mercy me. I kept my eyes on his boots, his shiny crocodile riding boots, the same ones he wore the first time I bumped into him up at the 40th street trail. City slicker I had nicknamed him then.

"Fiat, are you okay?"

My lips, independently from my brain, kept doing their open and close exercise while my hand shook out of control.

Brenda didn't waste any time. She grabbed hold of the Dane and said, "Let me guess, you were working on your Christmas cards... again."

I nodded, *thanks Aunt Brenda*, not. She turned and explained to Tristan about my 'Come to Arizona, the weather is so fine' ploy that I tried it on my family every Christmas. I'm not sure he paid much attention. His eyes were on my navel and once again, I tried to shield the view with my hand. It only made it more obvious, and I could see a devilish smile spreading from his amber eyes to his lips. Mr. Dumont was having a hell of a good time at my expense. What was he doing here?

"I – I –" I looked at Brenda, too embarrassed to glance in his direction.

"Monica, why don't you go get dressed? I think you skinned your rump. And take Dior with you. I'll be done in a minute."

Even if her words sounded a bit cold, her tone of voice was sweet. She felt my embarrassment and probably decided I'd been punished enough already. I took over Dior's collar and headed back toward the deserted pool, nodding to Tristan while walking away. He called after me, "Hey, Fiat, please make sure to add me to the Christmas card list. I can't wait."

I kept on walking.

"Was that Tristan Dumont?" Kassandra, fully dressed, waited inside my place. "Look Monica, don't get mad but I mean, he's a client. A very important client. I didn't feel comfortable being seen in my bathing suit. It's not dignified, unless you're at the beach, of course."

I didn't answer. Brenda was right, my tailbone hurt and was probably bruised. To her credit, Kassandra brought in the props from the pool, including the bag of Jerky treats, now shredded as Dior sat on the floor gobbling them up as fast as he could. I scrambled to recoup as many as possible. All I needed was for the dog to get sick. What a disaster. Twenty minutes later the three of us walked into Brenda's kitchen through the back door. No traces of Tristan. I discreetly peeked out the window; no black SUV either. The house smelled good — home-cooked food good. How was it possible? Brenda just got home. I looked at her and noticed her new haircut. Well, good for her. Maybe she was finally coming out of her slump.

"Well, girls, I'm warming up the oven and heating a pot roast I cooked yesterday since I knew I'd be gone most of the morning. Monica, feel like setting the table? For four."

Four? Noooo. He was coming back?

I just looked at her.

"Bob may stop by," she said, smiling.

Oh, she knew exactly what she was doing, playing mind games with my heart. Kassandra didn't seem to know what to do with herself, so she refilled Dior's water dish.

"Nice place you have here, Ms. Baker."

Brenda waved her off. "Oh, please, call me Brenda, I feel old enough without the 'Ms.' How about a glass of wine?"

"That would be terrific." Kassandra paused, "Real wine, not jelly, right?"

"Monica? You're still doing that stupid jelly thing?" Brenda rolled her eyes.

The table looked quite nice, that was one thing I knew how to do right.

"What was Tristan Dumont doing here?" I managed to say the whole sentence without stopping to gasp for air, not a small feat where Tristan was involved.

"Oh, we ran into each other at the 40th street signal, and we were talking while waiting for the light to change. It felt sort of natural for him to follow me. He gave me a copy of the proposal for the Dumont Foundation he is setting up and offered me a seat on the board. It's a great project. The City of Tucson is getting involved. You have no clue what I'm talking about, do you?"

I shook my head.

"Has to do with the Ranch he's purchased. You know about the horse sanctuary. Well they are adding a small condo project for retired ranch hands and farmers on low incomes. The county will help with the construction, and the retirees will work with the horses to make up for part of the rent. Look, I need to really assimilate everything he has given me. It's not something to be taken lightly." She checked her watch, "Fifteen minutes and we eat. I'll make a salad. Hey Kassandra, did you find the wine?"

Brenda paused and looked at me, I mean, there was something in her eyes that made me feel like I had done something wrong.

"How long has this been going on?" she asked.

I could feel Kassandra behind me, listening.

"Is that why I haven't seen Max around lately?"

"What the hell are you talking about? Max is in Telluride with his parents. They own a condo there. Anyway he's a friend, not my husband."

My tone a tad too loud for a guilt-free conversation. Again, I felt that sense of unease deep down inside. Guilt about what?

"You noticed it too?" Kassandra spoke from the kitchen door. "It's the same at the office," she quipped, "The minute he comes through the door, his eyes are searching and she's hiding in her cubicle or rushing out to run 'errands.' It's sort of cute, as in high school crush cute."

OMG! They were talking about me and – Tristan. No, no. So wrong. "What's wrong with you people? The man is married. M-a-r-r-i-e-d. Get it?" I was so angry I wanted to hurt them, to make my own hurt go away.

"Monica, are you talking about Angelique?"

I shook my head yes and avoided looking at Brenda. The oven timer went off and the three of us just stood there, the only sound was that of Dior crunching his kibble. "Look, I know Tristan's private on the subject of his wife, but certainly he must have shared something with you."

I felt anger and sadness rise in my chest, how dare these women assume that Tristan shared his marital life with me. Or did he? That 'important' message Tristan had emailed me that day after I visited him, the one I deleted without reading it because... because... I couldn't for the life of me remember what compelled me to do that. And what if indeed that was Tristan's way of opening up to me?

A light knock at the front door.

"Must be Bob. Let me get the meat from the oven before I burn everything. Kassandra, can you get the door? Monica, I think you should freshen up a little, you look like you've been watching a sad movie. No crying on my china," she teased and disappeared into the kitchen. I couldn't move. Dior toddled along with Kassandra to the front door.

"Well, well," a woman's voice. "What a surprise. We are looking for Brenda Baker." I moved toward the open door where stood Adam and Eve, the couple of detectives I met that evening at the office. The she-cop with her fake smile.

The Homicide Detectives.

Looking for Aunt Brenda.

SIX

I ate my cold lunch and cried in my $1 white dinner plate purchased at last year's January sale at Big Lots. Big Lots closed their doors a few months later so this felt like a relic.

Not the way I had envisioned spending my Saturday. What a disappointment. After the two detectives politely invited Brenda to go to the precinct to look at some camera footage, they asked Kassandra to join the party. Since she was a regular at the Psychic Fairs, they concluded she might recognize some of the people who came in contact with Miss Fortune. Before she headed out, Brenda insisted I help myself to the food and to please keep an eye on Dior. She spoke while carefully avoiding looking at me as Officer Clarke, AKA Bob to his friends, showed up and offered to take Brenda to the station. Kassandra drove her own car, and Dior and I came back to my place with a plate full of cold pot roast. And my mind full of self-pity.

Too much to digest, and no, nothing to do with the leftovers. First, Tristan showed up for no apparent reason. I simply couldn't accept Brenda's explanation and then — then I found out Brenda had gone to the fair. *The Psychic Fair*. How could she? She never, ever told me a thing about it. I tried to recall our precise conversation that day when she claimed she read about it in the newspaper. Yeah, sure, before or after she paid for reserving a spot. A spot for what? A séance? An astrological chart? Or that thing — the aura reading. Someone at the office was talking about that.

Apparently, everyone I knew was somehow connected to the fair, except me, of course. How about Tristan? Was that what he was discussing with Brenda? All the suspicions and hurtful questions gave me a headache. And Dior was getting restless.

"Hey big boy, how about we go for a walk? What do you say?" My first instinct was to hit 40th street, on the horse trails. And, no, I wasn't going to go chasing Tristan Dumont until Brenda spilled what she knew about Angelique. Finally, a wise decision.

"Okay Dior, we'll do the neighborhood. We need to be back here when your mom comes home so I can get all the dirty details. Don't look at me like that. It's not my fault. They started it." *They? Discussing my problems with a dog?*

I grabbed the leash and Dior got excited. I slipped a poop baggie in my jeans pocket and hit the street. Brenda's Pilot was still parked in the same spot where she left it when she got home. Such an odd sight. Across the street the neighborhood widow was busy watering something with her hose. She waved with her free hand. Probably dying to find out what was going on. Cars coming and going, especially Officer Clarke, whom she must remember from the break-in back in November. I quickened my steps, not in a chatting mood. Apparently neither was Dior and soon he was ahead, dragging me along. We turned North on 36th street. With such a mild winter, I didn't even need a jacket until the sun went down. I'd bet Phoenix, in particular, and Arizona in general, were the envy of 90% of the United States.

The fast pace felt like a soothing balm to my soul. Instead of anger, my thoughts shifted to Tristan's last words.

"Hey, Fiat, please make sure to add me to the Christmas card list. I can't wait."

In retrospect, he sounded so sweet... and looked just... yummy. Stop it Monica. That's when I realized I'd left my cell at home. I'd no clue how long we had been walking, but Dior decided to drink from someone's sprinklers. Two doors down, he serendipitously lifted his leg on someone's rose bushes. Yep. Time to take a different route home, pronto.

The widow was still outside, minus the hose. She crossed the road, and there was no avoiding her. "You just missed Tommy, your ex," she said.

"Oh." I pulled back on Dior. The big goof loved to go hopping around the poor woman, I blamed her heavy perfume, but honestly had no idea why Dior acted so naughty at times.

"He was disappointed that no one was home and I suppose a little puzzled that your aunt Brenda would leave her car at the curb." She waited for my response.

"Yep, no clue why she would do that." I shrugged. "We'll find out when she gets back, I guess." And with that I hastily walked up the driveway before she had a chance to ask more questions, especially since I had no real answers. I unlocked my door just as my cell stopped chiming. Damn. Dior didn't give me a chance to see whose call I missed. He headed back out the door, and I barely caught his leash just as Brenda's Honda inched up the driveway.

Talk about timing. How did she get there so fast without me seeing her? The answer came walking up right behind the SUV. Hello Officer Bob Clarke. We smiled at each other while I waited for Brenda to get out of the garage, handed her Dior's leash, and said, "Hello and good bye. I'm going to settle in for the evening. I'm sure anything new can wait."

I may have been wrong, but I swear, both sighed in relief as they disappeared into the house through the back entrance. I locked my front door behind me, kicked off my shoes and went to check the phone.

I had a voicemail from Max; it could wait. An angry, "Where the f**k is everybody?" from Tommy, and a missed call from Kassandra. I poured myself a glass of sparkling Prosecco, stretched out on my unmade bed and dialed her number.

"Hey, about time, where were you?" she asked.

"Took Dior for a walk. I had to. Needed some fresh air. I'm drowning in lies and deception. I still can't get over it. Brenda went to the fair. Unbelievable. What else is she hiding and lying about and ..."

"Oh, zip it, Ms. Drama Queen. It's not what you think. I'm spent. I came straight home, well, picked up a pizza to go, and I'm sitting comfortably eating greasy pepperoni and drinking a cold brew. Yeah. I suggest you make yourself comfy, too, because if you think what your aunt did is strange, well, you haven't heard the rest. Guess who else went to the fair?"

She must have swallowed her cold brew down the wrong pipe because she started to cough and spit. In between all that she chuckled. Damn. I was dying to know... and couldn't stop my one-track mind from spelling Tristan's name in flashing lights and bright colors. Mercy me. Kassandra finally calmed down.

"By the way, it's better than a movie, the way they have this stuff set up at the police place. Except for the popcorn. We all sat and watched the security footage on big screens with a tech standing by and ready to magnify rewind. Whatever it is they do. It pretty much showed that neither your aunt nor I are involved. And the detectives believe us now. Anyway, that's the way I see it. What do you think?"

"You're older, you know better. How about you tell me what you saw? Details and all." I couldn't choke back the edge in my voice.

"Calm down. You've been a pain ever since Pretty Boy Dumont showed up to photobomb your Christmas cards. Anyway, you ought to be proud of Brenda. Guess why she went to the Psychic Fair? To consult with that celebrity I wanted to meet. Remember? The Energy Therapist? It did take spunk at her age and never, ever, having done anything like that before. Anyway, she signed up for his six-month program to help with her anxiety, emotional issues and to rebalance her energy to resolve her weight issues. I wish I could afford that."

"Why? You have weight issues?" Make *snarky* my middle name. "Sorry, Kassandra. I'm mad at myself and taking it out on you."

She chuckled, "I'll forgive you because I'm in a good mood. I shouldn't be, but I am. Listen, Miss Fortune was in the security camera footage. She stopped at the booth that sells stones and crystals. We all know the owner, Jill. She's missed a few fairs because of her health so it was good seeing her smile. Brenda was at the same booth, checking out some of the crystals when Miss Fortune stopped to say hello to Jill. There was a brief exchange among the three women, but it was obvious that Brenda didn't really know either of them. Then Miss Fortune stepped away and called my number."

"You can actually see her dialing your number?"

"Huh, I didn't think about that. The tech said they never did find her phone or her bag but they have the list of numbers called from her service provider. They compared them with my phone and the times correspond. Isn't that weird? She called my number, standing a few feet from Brenda."

I could hear her munching. I had to admit, that detail gave me goose bumps, and I didn't even know the poor woman.

"Then a man caught up to Miss Fortune. I could only see the back of his head, but he looked somewhat familiar. Reminded me of that creep, you know, the homeowner where we had the séance?"

"Oh, no. The one who assaulted you? You left your bra in his house. That's it. He's the one, right? What's his name?" Why was I getting all worked up over this? Nothing could change the outcome. Miss Fortune was gone. How sad.

"Bill Smith." Sadness muffled Kassandra's voice. "That was the name on his Facebook page. I had the directions to his house on my phone, so I hope that helps. I wish I'd seen his face on the footage, just to be sure. Poor Miss Fortune. I feel so bad about it. The good thing is that both Brenda and I are pretty much in the clear and out of the picture. Oh, talking about being out of the picture. Are you sitting down?"

"Umm, yeah. Why? What else happened?"

"We were getting up from our chairs to leave, the camera was still rolling and you could see Jill's booth with all the pretty crystals and a few wind chimes when... pay attention... Celine enters the picture."

"Wait... what? Celine as in Sunny's daughter? Nooo. Was she with Brenda?"

"No, I told you to pay attention. This is more fun than musical chairs. Brenda had left, Miss Fortune and the man were chatting in the background when Celine appeared. Looked like she had some papers rolled up. Maybe a picture of her aura? I don't know. She put her purse on the counter to check out a crystal on a chain and she had a little bag sticking out of her purse. I know I've seen those cute paper bags before but can't remember where. I couldn't help myself, I called out her name. Brenda turned around and recognized Celine, too. She was a lot more surprised than I was."

I gulped down my Prosecco and declared, "Apparently everyone I know was at the fair, except me."

"Hey, miss poor me," Kassandra scolded, "I wasn't there in person, either. Stop whining."

That didn't help my mood but I let it go. "What's the name of the creep again? Bill Smith? How original. I'm going to look him up online and see what he looks like."

"Too late," she said. "I already checked, first thing I did when I got home. His Facebook page is gone. Poof. Oh, there are plenty of Bill Smiths. I bet they are all phony names, as his probably was. But the detectives have all the information I could think of and I'm sure Mr. Zuckerberg will gladly let them search through old files if it helps to catch a murderer. Right?" Now she sounded as snarky as I did.

"Right." I said, returning the snark. I got off the bed to double-check the locks on all my doors and windows.

SEVEN

Didn't know when Bob Clarke went home. *If* he went home. I fell asleep watching some boring rerun. The television was still on when I woke up. Or to be precise, when a loud knocking at my door woke me up. The light filtering from the mini blinds provided a sense of safety when I opened the door without even asking who it was. And I was still wearing my sweats from walking Dior the day before. Great.

"Hey, good morning." Brenda, fully dressed and even sporting a hint of lipstick, handed me a mug of steaming coffee. "And you're already dressed." She sounded sincere, not mocking me in the least. "I slept with my clothes on," I confessed.

"Are you working today?" There we stood, like two polite strangers, exchanging meaningless niceties... so wrong. I shook my head no. "No more open houses until after Christmas. Kay says buyers and sellers have other priorities right now. I tend to agree."

Brenda kept nodding. The mug felt hot against my fingers, I didn't know what to do with myself. I could hear Dior barking by the back door. And I was dying to ask about Officer Clarke but a little voice in my head told me not to. I heeded the voice.

Did Brenda sense my edginess? She reached out and patted my arm. A feeling of serenity and acceptance exuded from her touch. I'm ashamed to say my first reaction was, "Oh, she got some last night." I immediately regretted it and hoped with all my might she couldn't read my mind.

"Monica, relax. Bob isn't here." Ouch. Mind reader? "He's my friend, not my boyfriend." Her eyes searched mine; I nodded. Well at this point I couldn't care if she had sex or if the Energy Therapist was a wizard; something about Aunt Brenda was different, in a major way, in a wonderful way. I followed her back to her house. Her pack of smokes sat at the usual spot, but I couldn't see any forbidden junk foods. The place smelled of scrambled eggs and bacon, and I had to assume the bacon was real and she'd already cooked it because Dior circled the kitchen with fierce determination. *Happy days are here again.*

We ate breakfast together. Brenda was ripping ads from the Sunday's paper insert. "I need a dress, something black, simple, that I can wear to both my work Christmas dinner and a party at Bob's office."

"Wow, you have twice the social life I have. My Sunday afternoon is yours. If you want, we can try the Mall or you may even like Stein Mart, across the street from the mall. I found a real cute top at half price."

"That'll be fun. If we're lucky, we'll make it out of here before Tommy shows up with another one of his sad stories. By the way, that Kassandra is a riot, isn't she? The way she described the usual participants at Psychic Fairs, she had the detectives in stiches." She paused. My turn to redeem myself.

"She had nothing but good things to say about the — about the therapist you are working with. She had told me he was a celebrity in the world of psychics, the ones with real degrees, I mean." I stopped. Brenda smiled at me. Whoa, I felt like a mountain of worries just rolled off my back.

"How about we leave around one o'clock. I'll drive. And, remind me to share what little I know about Angelique."

I've no clue how I made it to one o'clock without calling Kassandra or wearing out the floor where I paced back and forth to kill time. While the changes in Brenda were all super positives, I missed her snarky attitude. Again that little voice in my head told me to wait. I was getting used to that voice – maybe it was called maturity?

Brenda did find her dress at Stein Mart and only needed one size larger than usual. Interesting. Maybe she had already dropped some inches. I proudly flashed the email offering a 10% discount I'd received on my phone for being a Stein Mart subscriber.

The collective sense of urgency that seems to permeate shoppers when December hits was alive and well in every parking lot, every store, big or small. As the sun started to set, the holiday lights came on, giving even gas stations a festive look. It all begged for a happy hour detour to end our day gloriously and — to speak 'Angelique' in a public place where I couldn't possibly make a fool of myself, right?

While we were both intrigued by *The Covenant*, a brand new restaurant that replaced the old vitamin store at the corner of Shea and Tatum, we headed to Z'Tejas where the covered patio seemed to hold the answer to our immediate mood, and the appetizers and drinks held no secrets after all our frequent visits over the years. We left Brenda's purchases in her Honda and sat in the smoking section of the narrow, outside patio, with a great view of the busy surroundings. Brenda's hand riffled in her bag before her derriere fully adjusted to the rattan chair. Cigarettes. Her tension was readable.

"I left my smokes home," she said. "On purpose." The hand on the table shook. "Maybe I'm pushing too hard. I'm setting myself up for failure."

I searched for words of comfort, found none. This was supposed to be my time. My moment of happy discovery when Brenda would tell me that there was no marriage. Angelique was Tristan's stepmother, or his aunt, or anything but his wife. Scenes reminiscent of old movies with young women having to give up the man they loved to marry the old rich man chosen by her impoverished family flashed through my mind in spite the fact there was no correlation with anything related to the Dumont's marital status. Meantime, Brenda's nicotine needs reached the drama status. Tension must be contagious. I found myself shaking.

"Brenda." I breathed deeply. "I think we should get up and drive home. We'll be there in five minutes. You can have a cigarette and we can share a glass of wine and a piece of cheese so we don't mess with all that you've accomplished so far."

At first she just blinked, then it must have sunk in. She stood, still visibly shaken, turned to the smiling waitress heading our way. "Miss, I'm so sorry. We have an emergency; we must leave. Please excuse us." She laid a $5 bill on the table and pushed me toward the small gate opening onto the street. We drove in silence.

About six minutes later, Brenda lit her cigarette. She blew the first puff of smoke with the same expression I probably wore after a particularly satisfying orgasm. I went to the kitchen to get a bottle of Pinot Grigio from her refrigerator. I had to get the right mood back for our Angelique chat. That's probably where I was when Bob Clarke knocked on the door. When I got back with the two stem glasses he was discussing Christmas lights for Brenda's front yard Palo Verde tree.

He nodded at me. I rested the Pinot and the glasses on the low table by the couch, picked up my purse and headed home. I doubt Brenda even noticed my exit. And Dior seemed as bamboozled by Bob as Brenda was. I suspected Bob of using that bacon trick like Jack Nicholson in the movie *As Good as it Gets*; not that it really mattered at this point.

EIGHT

M is for Monica, and also for moody.

M is for Monday. Make that a double M, for Monday Morning. Put it all together and what do you get? Monica is moody because it's Monday morning. The end. Well, not really. More like the beginning of a new week. And what a way to start the week. I don't know why but I found myself driving south on the 51 instead of Tatum Boulevard.

On a Monday morning. Shoot me now.

Everything was going south, not just me. My Fiat didn't handle as smoothly as usual. Maybe it's true that we attract what we project. I read that in a book. So now my car acted moody, just like me. I got off on Glendale Avenue and drove surface streets to the office where I parked next to Scott's truck.

"Morning Scott. Lots of new listings?" Scott was in charge of installing and removing our real estate signs.

He looked at me the way I look at bugs. "New listings? It's December. I'm taking the rest of the month off. I'm going to Utah, skiing." Then he did something rather peculiar, even for an odd guy like Scott. He walked to the back of my car and kicked my tire. "You need to get your tire fixed. This one is flat. How long have you been driving on a flat tire?"

"Flat tire?" I echoed. That explained why I had trouble driving. Ah. Damn Mondays!

Scott watched me squat down to check out the tire, or at least pretend I did. It looked a bit out of air, but flat? Except, it seemed to get flatter as I watched. I grabbed my stuff, "Thanks. I'll call AAA. I have a spare."

If he heard me he didn't care. He kept rearranging the white wooden posts on the back of the truck. Skiing in Utah. Hard to imagine snow in the next state when it was like late spring weather in Phoenix. Max was supposed to be skiing in Telluride. Good for him. I grew up in the Italian Dolomites and ski slopes were only about thirty minutes from home. Even so, I had never had any interest in skiing. However, I did like the après ski. Liked it? Loved it. All the fun without huffing and puffing to get to the top of crowded slopes. The fun memories put a smile in my heart and a skip in my steps. Inside, the office was busy. Or maybe it looked that way because more agents sat around the bullpen and chatted now that sellers didn't want us in their homes.

"Hi, Kassandra." I bypassed her desk and headed straight for the kitchen and the coffee maker.

"Monica, someone called about your appointment for a photo shoot. You have a new listing you forgot to enter in the system."

"Oh, no, no. I'm following Kay's suggestion. Yes, we are taking pictures, lots of pictures and I'll probably list the property by the end of the week. Oh, Scott just told me he's taking time off and going skiing in Utah. What am I going to do about the post and the sign?"

"Don't pay too much attention to Scott. He did the same thing last year. He was back in the office after the second day. Too cold," she snickered.

"You talking about me again?" Scott stood by the front door, looking more bored than upset. "I've got to go to pick up a sign in Scottsdale. Do you want me to move it over to your new listing?" he asked.

"Oh, that's so nice of you, but it's a gated community, and I need to get the okay from the HOA before I do anything," I said.

He shrugged. "Don't forget your tire." He turned around and left.

"What's wrong with your tire?" Kassandra asked.

My coffee was getting cold. "My rear tire went flat. I'm going to my cubicle and call AAA; they are really good about it. Hey, want to stop for a *chat* after work?" I winked at her, she knew I meant drink. Her big grin was a yes.

I could see Sunny in her glass domain, talking on the phone. I was curious to know if Kassandra had told Sunny about Celine's presence at the Physic Fair. It ought to be interesting. The bad feeling brought on by Brenda's dismissal of our planned and highly anticipated chat about Tristan in favor of an evening with Bob Clarke still lingered, but not as strong. Plus, I had to get the tire taken care of, my appointment with the photographer was in one hour, and it was too late to reschedule. I pulled out my AAA card from my wallet and dialed. I made the mistake of telling the road assistance operator I wasn't in any danger, but sitting comfortably in my office, so my call wasn't entered as an emergency. Damn. And it was Monday.

I was too fidgety to sit back and twiddle my thumbs. Might as well get my files organized. Checked my SupraBox key container. Okay it wasn't mine. Sunny loaned it to me, but the eKey was all mine, bought and paid for with my first commission. I checked, fully charged. Each time an iBox is opened, both the key and iBox record the date, time and the identity of the key holder. That's why I had to have my own. Sunny had warned me, "Guard it with your life." I had memorized my code and plugged the eKey in every evening, whether I had used it or not.

Kay's office door was closed. That explained why I didn't see her car in the parking lot. Time moved slowly, too slowly. I needed to get on the road in about fifteen minutes in order to make it to the Scottsdale listing in plenty of time. I called the AAA road service number again, got a different operator and explained my problem. Only to be told that it would be another twenty minutes before their technician got to me. Rats. I couldn't sit still. I walked back to the kitchen, rinsed out my mug and put it back on the shelf.

"What's with you?" Not much got by Kassandra. Probably why everyone liked her. I told her about my conversation with AAA.

"You're not picking up clients, just meeting the photographer, right?"

"No. No clients, and the home we are photographing is vacant. The owners left a few pieces of furniture so we can do a little staging for the photos. Makes the rooms look better, you know." I kept an even tone, but inside I was screaming to get on the road.

"Here." Kassandra handed me a key.

"What is this for?"

"The key to my Kia. Just take it. Get the photos done and then bring it back. Leave me your keys and your AAA card. By the time you're back your tire will be replaced. Now stop hyperventilating. You're stressing me out.'

"Huh, I — you're sure?"

"Really Monica, my car is a piece of crap, but it will get you there and if you really feel like you owe me, put some gas in the tank. It's unlocked. Go, already, go. No speeding, you hear me?"

I felt overwhelmed by her kindness. Or maybe it was something I ate. Fill her tank, yes, that's what I would do. I thanked her again, took the key and left.

Too late for breakfast and too early for lunch, so where were all those slow pokes going? Some crossed the road while smoking and holding a Styrofoam cup of something. Of course, mid-morning break for office folks on salaries. Not something people on commission, like realtors, get to enjoy. *Breathe Monica, breathe and stop bitching.*

Kassandra's car made some funky noises. *Pong, pong, grind, pong.* The series of sounds recurred at precise intervals almost like a refrain in a song. Maybe I should stop by a gas station. There was one up the road. I pushed the gas pedal. Time wasn't on my side. I made a quick right, cutting off a mud-covered SUV full of kids. I kept my eyes focused straight ahead in case one of the SUV's occupants used fingers signs. I made it to the gas station without too much fuss. It only had four gas pumps and a line of waiting cars for every one of them. Darn Mondays. What now?

Only twenty minutes left. I looked around to assess the situation without pissing off another overworked, driving mother. But hey, I had plenty of gas, I could always fill the tank on my way back. I drove to the end of the pump island and then made an attempt at a U-turn on a squeal of tires. No, not the Kia's tires. The ones on a beat up camper truck that barely missed me. I could see from the corner of my eye the angry driver rolling down the window. Mercy me. Not now. I drove south, staying close to the sidewalk and when I saw an opening onto traffic I made a wide U-turn and headed north. I barely cleared the intersection as the light turned red. Good.

I mentally patted myself on the back until I checked my rear view mirror. Nooo. The unmistakable crappy silhouette of the camper from hell was pursuing the Kia and gaining ground. All of this on a stretch of Camelback Road sided by hotels that made the list of favorite places of the rich and famous every year. Few cars on the road and absolutely no soul on foot. The grimy, old camper getting closer and closer and the 'Objects in mirror are closer than they appear' engraved on the side mirror was giving me the willies.

This is Phoenix, the wild, wild west. People have guns. People with campers may even have shotguns and not be afraid to use them. I tried to drive with an eye on the camper. Like all Arizona vehicles, it didn't have a front license plate, and then, just like that, I hit a red light and came to a screeching halt. The camper crept slowly next to me, and the driver got out. My hands shook so bad, I tried to remember what I used to say in Italian when the cops pulled me over, but my brain wasn't cooperating. Plus, what if he mistook me for an illegal and he was one of those 'This is America, speak English' kind of guys. Ouch.

He made it to the passenger side before I could spell C I A O in my mind. There was nothing threatening in his attitude. He had a stubby face with strange glasses, like reading glasses with those darker clip-ons people wear when it's sunny. He knocked on the passenger window and in my spur of the moment lack of common sense I rolled it down. Yes, I had to manually open it. He checked me out, taking his time.

"Hello," I said and waited.

Head cocked, he looked me over again, took a step closer to the window.

"Young lady, you need to be careful. We could have both been killed back there when you made that U-turn. In a hurry?"

His attempt at friendliness while ogling the interior of the Kia earned him an F, but I felt a sense of relief.

"Huh, I'm sorry. I'm borrowing a friend's car and I'm not too familiar with it. And yes, I'm late to an appointment. Again, so sorry."

I rolled the window up, slowly, forcing him to step back. That was it. Not another word, he walked backward, his eyes on me. The light was green and I took off while he was getting back to his camper. It was crazy. The man didn't say anything mean and yet I felt frightened to the core. I drove the rest of the way checking the rear view mirror to see if he was tailing me. And just before I arrived at the last turn to the gated community, I made a slight detour to see if indeed he had followed me. This was a busy street, so I parked behind a house under construction and I could swear a camper like his drove by. I was so nervous I could hardly get the Kia's gear into drive. Finally the car moved and the noises begin to repeat, but after the latest encounter, it felt more like a lullaby.

I entered the gate code and watched with a great sense of relief the small, white van from the R.E. Assist service follow me in. The photographer had made it here first. Safe at last. Until I noticed who was at the wheel of the R.E. Assist van.

NINE

Jessica Smith, also known as J.S. Smith, or Jessie for short. The reporter from hell.

"What did you do, kidnap the photographer? What for? This house is vacant and as far as I know nothing nefarious ever happened here. Nothing to write about it."

"You're wrong about me, Monica. Cross my heart." She looked sadly pathetic saying that. "I'm the new hire and I'm here to photograph your listing."

She handed me a business card. I opened my mouth a few times, and squinted, too, pretending to seriously study the computer-generated business card.

"I got canned, again. So I figured I'll take this job. After all, I'm good at taking photos, had a lot of practice while working under cover for the *We Dig Deeper* magazine."

She shook her red mane and I sort of felt sorry for her, but it didn't last long. I went to unlock the front door while Jessie began to unload her equipment from the back of the van. I have to admit, it all looked legit.

"What happened to the regular guy? What's his name? Al?"

"Alan got married; he's on his honeymoon?"

She carried one of those things into the entrance. A tripod?

"Huh? Married? He must be seventy at least. Not that it matters of course. Now don't go out there screaming age discrimination."

"What age discrimination? He probably is seventy, but last time I checked there is no law against getting married at seventy."

"No, there isn't it." I sighed, and flashes of paler, thinner skin and Angelique's aging face raced through my mind. I doubted Mrs. Dumont was that old. I looked at J.S. who was looking at me. Couldn't help wondering if we shared the same brief insight but I'll never know for sure. While she walked around to familiarize herself with the floorplan I explored the closets and the pantry.

The home had that smell of shut-off, old places. It didn't matter that the house had been thoroughly cleaned and, thanks to our dry climate, no mold or mildew to be concerned about. But unless you used plug-in air fresheners overloaded with chemically-induced, icky odor cover-ups, you got old folks smell. Personally, I would take the stale smell over flowery air fresheners any day, for sure. But right this moment I went from room to room and opened the windows wide. In the pantry, I found some silk plants and a few old baskets that could be used as props. Nothing of great monetary or sentimental value because, as Kay always reminded me, you can't trust everyone. Since I was the key holder, it was my responsibility to keep the place safe.

"Before it hits the market, I want to come back and place some nice fluffy towels in the master bath," I said.

"Oh, any particular thing I should be aware of before shooting it?"

"Nah, it's just the walk-in bath tub. I've never seen one before, it looks odd."

"Let me see." J.S. followed me through the master bedroom and looked inside the empty tub.

"I see what you mean," she mused. "What happens if after you're in there, surrounded by water and bubbles, you need to go?"

I gave her a look.

"No, not to pee," she said quickly. "That's a no brainer. I'm thinking – number 2?"

We stared at each other. "Whoa, that could get messy quick," she snickered. "Gross."

I nodded. "It sucks to get old."

"You should talk, I'm probably five, six years older than you are." She turned, adjusted her camera and clicked a pic of me, standing by the walk in tub, with my mouth open as usual.

Two hours later she was done and packed, ready to go. I gave her all my info for R.E. Assist Company. Part of their service was to post the photos to the Internet, but I had to approve them first. When Jessica left she had my phone number, email, and, *nagging thought*, my realtor member number and password. I kept my fingers crossed behind my back while sharing the info. Although it was all very legit, the uncomfortable feeling wouldn't go away. I locked up the house and took the long way to the main gate. I wanted to see the community pool and the crafts room. To my surprise, I realized there was also a tennis court and a nine-hole golf course. Very nice, perfect for a retired couple, I assumed.

On the way back to the office, I stopped to top off the Kia's tank and the concern about sharing info with J.S. came nagging at me with renewed vigor. She had to have had my info before we met at the listing. I maintained an account with the company that employed her and she was waiting there for me. Certainly, she'd been briefed and supplied the necessary data. Why did she ask for it again?

What if Al wasn't on his honeymoon and J.S. being assigned to my account wasn't a coincidence? And what if I stopped making myself sick over that? Why would she care? Why? The name Tristan came to mind. Crystal clear. Mercy me, between the camper dude and the former reporter chick this was definitely an Excedrin kind of afternoon.

The minute I locked the Kia, my eyes went to the installed spare tire on my pink beauty. Yes. Thanks AAA. How could I ever give up my little Fiat? We had been through so much together. My high heels clicked toward the office entrance, the listing file proudly tucked under my arm and the Kia's keys jingling in my hand.

Slam! The hefty office door was pushed open so fast it hit me hard, and I found myself falling backward. I dropped the keys trying to grab the decorative metal handle. That was close. As I worked at catching my breath and my balance, a pissed off Celine hissed, "*You*. Get the hell out of my way."

And she stomped out in such a rage she even forgot to sashay her hips. What was going on? How did I miss her powder blue Sebring? Too busy looking at my pink chariot?

Kassandra was at my side, Sunny trailing by seconds, “I’m sorry Monica, are you okay?”

I was still too shaken up and frankly — stunned — even to spell out a few choice adjectives befitting that spoiled brat Celine. A little voice in my head told me she must have had a fight with her mother, and by her explosive exit, she lost the argument.

Kassandra collected her car keys from the travertine floor. Our eyes met and she winked at me. Oh, that must have been a juicy squabble between my boss and her blonde nitwit kid. More tattle for our happy hour chats. “It’s okay, Sunny. What’s wrong with Celine, that time of the month?”

She rolled her eyes, “With Celine every day that she doesn’t get her way is that time of the month.”

Poor woman. I headed over to my cubicle and noticed Kay’s office door open, so I adjusted my route and popped in to say hello and report on the progress.

Kay’s office was very small and windowless. Perhaps a closet in its past life? She’d had the place decorated in pale green and white, more beach house than Arizona office. The door was left open when she didn’t have guests so I poked my head in. Today her knitted sweater matched her chair pillows and set off her naturally silver hair. *If only I could look so chic when I’m her age...*

“Well, I hope this new photographer is as good as Al.” I put it out there and waited.

“New photographer? Why? What happened to Al?” *I knew it.*

I told her the whole story. Okay, I left out sixty percent of my suspicions and even with barely forty percent, I caught Kay looking at me like I was batty. She kept staring, at least I thought she was looking at me since I was the only one there. Then a smile spread from her eyes to the rest of her face, and she asked, "Wait, are we talking about that dingbat reporter who wrote all that garbage about Celine and that young man? Oh, now I remember, the redhead who showed up at your first open house. Right?"

I nodded yes so enthusiastically I feared my head would come unhinged and roll off my body. Kay was obviously agreeing with me about J.S. Smith. Finally. I felt vindicated. She picked up the phone.

"This is easy. The owner of the company is an old friend. Let's find out." She got a busy signal. "I'm curious, why is this S.J, J. S. whatever the name, always chasing you down? What is it she wants from you?"

I shrugged, "She's sort of stuck on Tris — Mr. Dumont."

"What? Her too?" *Her too? OMG, was I that transparent?* Kay's fingers tapped on her desk. She looked amused. "Oh, I guess you weren't here. You missed Celine's big drama scene. That poor Sunny. I don't know how she can put up with her. It's days like these I'm thankful I never had kids."

I cleared my throat, "What drama scene?"

"Celine went to some witchcraft thing. No, no, a fair. Yes, A Psychic Fair. That's what I heard. That's what we all heard, and I'm not sure what's the big deal except that the nitwit went there to buy a love potion."

She laughed openly, “A love potion. Unbelievable and I bet she gave it, or tried to give it to that Tristan Dumont. Apparently, it didn’t work.”

She covered her mouth with her free hand not to sound too — amused?

“She and the reporter should get together and compare notes.” The phone still in her hand, she checked her watch, “Oops. Got to go. Let’s get together as soon as you receive the download and we’ll get you set up with your listing. Don’t worry, I’ll talk to my friend and find out about that Smith woman.”

I went back to my cubicle. Celine and the Psychic Fair. Love potion Kay said. Was the whole office at the fair? No, what was I thinking? Kassandra said she didn’t go. Not so, she went but didn’t stay. And Brenda was my aunt. However, she didn’t have anything to do with Desert Homes Realty, right? I could sure use some Excedrin, no joke. The tiny counter that made up my desk had a few post-its stuck in the weirdest places. Must be Kassandra’s wicked sense of humor. I was dying to hear her version of the love potion. Why would Celine tell her mother about it?

Clear your mind Monica, none of your biz. I read my messages: a call from that legal firm, the one with the fancy pants Esquire who was working on the accident settlement. Made me feel funny to be part of it. Tristan’s intentions were good, I just didn’t know how I could claim damages. I was totally recovered and really, Tristan lost his Land Rover and spent weeks in a cast. Oh, well, later. A receipt from AAA, with a notation recommending I replace the tire, meaning buy a new one? Better make up my mind about my

Fiat. A folded white piece of paper, hand written in cursive? From Tristan? He was here? In my cubicle? Be still my heart. Maybe that's when Celine gave him the love potion? How? *Mouth to mouth?* Stop it Monica. I read the note.

Hey Fiat, noticed someone working on your car. Call me if you need a ride. Here is my cell #. T.

How sweet was that? He must have been here meeting with Sunny while AAA changed my tire. On impulse I held his note against my heart. Then looked around, no one saw me. Good. As if anyone cared about my romantic dreams. The office was very, very quiet. I could see Sunny in her glass office, talking on the phone and skimming through a thick file. It always amazed me to see how organized and focused she could be. Celine must take after her father, whoever he was.

I had a phone call from the couple who hired me to sell their house. I called them back and updated them on the progress. I also promised to let them see the photos before the rest of the world did. They sounded pretty excited, especially the wife who loved the new living arrangements, adding she no longer had to cook. They ate their main meals in the elegant restaurant and, of course, the food had to be fantastic. After all, Brenda was in charge of the menu. Sunny was leaving with a stack of files under her arm. She gave me a thumbs up, without slowing her pace.

"We have a closing date."

No need to explain. My heart summersaulted. We were closing Tristan's horse ranch in Tucson. Bittersweet news. I was about to get a nice chunk of money. Then again, this meant the end of my business-related connection with Dumont.

"Why the sad face?"

I didn't hear Kassandra sneaking up on me.

"Everyone is gone. Get your stuff and I'll switch the phones to the answering service. Let's go party," she said with a wicked grin.

"Seriously Kassandra? It's Monday. Tomorrow morning we are back here."

"Aren't you a barrel of fun? Let's go somewhere with outside tables, and I don't mean North Italia. Somewhere with loud people and music. You are not going to believe what I found out today. Let's go. You've got ten minutes to get to your car before I set the alarm."

She turned around and left me there wondering what had she been doing. Bathing in Red Bull?

Seven minutes later I unlocked my Fiat 500. What was that old saying? "Curiosity killed the cat?" No cat here, just Monica Baker, dying of curiosity.

TEN

"I need to get back to my tarot cards. Every morning, before starting the day, I would pull a random card from the stack. It helped me mentally. Haven't done that in a while and now my whole life is going down the toilet."

This from the girlfriend who demanded a place with loud people and music and outside tables, etc. Wow! What's next? Crying in her drink? "I never pulled any card," I said, "and my life isn't any smoother than yours right now. But what happened with Celine?"

How did we end up here anyhow? I had no idea El Chorro offered happy hours. Of course it wasn't like the happy hours we were familiar with. I did get a glass of generic white wine at a reasonable price, but the food was a little too upscale right at this moment. I couldn't even pronounce some of the items on the menu. And even the building was different. Bigger? More modern? I couldn't be sure. The only other time I'd been there was with Tommy, my ex, and we were newlyweds. While I perused the architectural wonders of the lodge, Kassandra ordered a dirty martini. Not a good thing. I finally settled on my go-to when in doubt: Calamari, hold the sauce, lots of lemon.

"Oh, that bimbo in high heels." She wiped olive juice from her lips. "She showed up on Dumont's trail, as usual. Somehow she didn't find him right away. I don't know, maybe he used the john. Eventually she chased him to the parking lot but he drove off. I assume she then noticed your can of Pepto-Bismol parked there, and no trace of you at the office. Of course, I wasn't about to volunteer that you borrowed my car." She giggled. "Way too much fun to watch her come unglued. I knew she had visited the fair, and had suspicions about why, but kept it to myself. Then while she's looking around to see who she can harass next, her mother summons her to her office and before the door closed on her sweet cheeks, I heard something about 'you at the Psychic fair.' I swear, she didn't get it from me." She gulped down her martini.

Too embarrassed to ask why her cocktail was called dirty, I focused on squeezing lemon wedges on my calamari when she ordered another martini. "Kassandra, you are eating olives and drinking hard liquor. You won't be able to drive home."

"It's okay, my Kia is like a horse; she'll take me home, no problem."

"Yes. Problem. For starters, we are in Paradise Valley, with the most organized and effective police force. Seriously, why are you drinking so much? What happened while I was gone from the office?"

"Aren't you the cutest little curious Italian?" She reached over to poke me and spilled her drink all over the table. I took that as a blessing until the waiter who had been circling the table ever since we got there with his eyes on Kassandra, hurried over and brought another martini. Courtesy of the house, he said. Or something just as stupid. Kassandra didn't hear him.

She was head down trying to find the olive that had rolled under the table.

"That's it," I said. "Get up, I'm driving you home. We'll leave your car here. You can get it in the morning. I'll talk to the manager."

"No one goes home with me, no one." Was she crying? "It's all my fault. Poor Miss Fortune. No, no, not Fortune her name is — was — Peg. Peg Campos. I like Fortune better; what do you think, Monica?"

"I think that it's time to go. Can you walk? No, wait. Let me go pay and make sure we can leave the Kia parked overnight. Do you need to get something from the car? Is it locked? Damn, I don't even know where you live."

"I'm not telling you." She reached over and grabbed my glass, drinking whatever little was left. "Everybody lies. That Bill Smith lied. He didn't even live in the house where I left my bra." Kassandra was getting louder and louder. Well, we did accomplish something. We were in a place with loud people, that's for sure. I left her at the table, mumbling to herself and went to pay the bill. I asked if I could leave Kassandra's vehicle there. The answer was yes but the whole compound would be locked up until around eight a.m.

I didn't care; anything was better than Kassandra attempting to drive home. I still couldn't understand how she got drunk so fast. Unless she was already drinking at the office.

Getting her to sit in my Fiat was another chore. I pushed the passenger seat as far back as possible. Her breath reeked of those awful liquid cough medicines that make you drowsy. I drove out of El Chorro parking lot and all the way to the shopping center on the corner of 32nd St. and Lincoln. The first place where I could park and talk to Kassandra without risking a fine. I needed to find out her address. I managed to wrestle her handbag away from her and pulled out her wallet. I figured the safest thing was to look at her address on her driver's license. I kept the windows open, praying she didn't throw up.

Luckily, she nodded off when the Fiat started rolling. All the months I'd been at Desert Homes Realty and the many happy hours Kassandra and I had spent together, I had never, ever seen her so wasted. Something must have happened, besides finding out Miss Fortune's real name. Kassandra's address on her driver's license said Scottsdale. Scottsdale? She told me she lived around Seventh Avenue and Northern. Then I understood. She never changed the address at the DMV. What now?

"Kassandra, what's the name of the complex where you live?"

She twitched the left side of her mouth, licked off some drool. "Live? Who? We all die, don't you know?"

"Kassandra, don't go back to sleep. It's me, Monica." I shook her shoulder while she tried to wiggle away. Thank god it was dark enough so even a passerby couldn't see what was going on in the car. "Your condo, where is it? What is the place called?"

"The happiest place on earth." She hummed the Disney jingle. My patience was running short. I wasn't good when it came to reasoning with stubborn adults.

"Pay attention. When you go home, what does the sign on the entrance of the complex say?"

"Monica, you're sooo funny. Signs don't talk."

"True, true, but people do. So talk to me and tell me where your condo is. Okay?"

"Okay. It's easy to find, on the corner of seventh and Northern. That's why it's called Northern Star. See? On Northern, the star."

She kept on babbling and pointing to the dark sky while I quickly entered the name on my phone. Sure enough, the map showed we were close. Finally, something positive. I put the Fiat in gear and headed West on Lincoln that quickly became Glendale Avenue once we entered Phoenix.

The complex was well lit and looked rather nice but deserted. I had no idea where to go. The leasing office was obviously closed. How was I going to figure out which of the two three-story buildings was Kassandra's?

"He even remembered the building," she said, out of the blue. "He said it makes sense. It's Building A because I'm definitely an A. And he wasn't talking about my cup size."

She laughed out loud. I veered right to Building A. Progress. Now I needed a floor and then an apartment number. I headed to a parking spot marked Guest when Kassandra said, "It's better if you park on that other guest parking; it's closer to my condo." Bingo.

Maybe the alcohol was wearing off because five minutes later she handed me her car keys with her condo key attached. Building A, second floor, apartment number 19. I offered to help her get into bed. She answered by rolling her eyes at me. Good. That was the real Kassandra. She wasn't going to bed.

She said her head felt funny, and she was allergic to hard liquor.

When I left she was brewing herself tea in her spotless, white kitchen. I would be back in the morning around eight so we could get her Kia and she could still make it to the office by eighth-thirty.

It was barely eight p.m. by the time I hit Shea Boulevard but it felt more like midnight. And to say that the evening had been fun would be like saying that the bulls volunteer their time in the arena. On the way home, my stomach kept rumbling and I kept remembering all that mumble-jumble Kassandra kept spewing about living and dying and the man saying Building A, but none of it made any sense. Better clear my mind and hope I could steal some food from Brenda. What if Officer Clarke was there? Well, better practice calling him Bob because I wasn't about to keep on missing meals due to his frequent visits. How long was she going to drag out the 'we are just friends' charade?

All the lights were on at Brenda's place, and I mean all of them, porch lights, front lawn lights. You get the idea. What was going on? I knew what wasn't going on... hanky panky or cooking. My stomach had been grumbling loudly for the last thirty minutes. I drove up the driveway. Brenda and I parked our cars in the same building, but a center wall divided the two parking stalls. We each had our own garage door with electric opener. From her side she could get to her house though her laundry room. On my side I had access to my smaller place through my kitchen. In general, it was a convenient solution, except for tonight. Her garage door was up and her Honda Pilot was parked half in the garage and half sticking out on the driveway. So it would be a little tight for me to get to my garage, but okay. Not the first time. And here in the back all the lights were also on.

Dior must have heard my car. He was barking and pushing against the screen door. Where was Brenda? Would this night ever get back to normal? I squeezed my Fiat into my space, my eyes pausing on the spare tire as I got out. I hoped it would hold up until I got Kassandra back to El Chorro to get her Kia. How did I get myself into such idiotic situations? I clicked my garage closed and marched over to Brenda's back door.

"Okay, okay Dior, I love you too. Where is your mama?"

"In here." Brenda's voice came from her to-die-for pantry. That's where she usually retreated when planning a large catering event. Something that hadn't happened since her hospital stay due to her near fatal overdose of sleeping pills. Maybe the night was about to get better. "What's up?" I asked. "You got a new gig? Where? How big?"

"Not yet little girl, but getting there."

I smiled, remembering the last time Brenda called me little girl. Aunt Brenda was back, or close to it and I didn't see Officer Clarke, *Bob to his friends,* anywhere around. Maybe things were improving all around. "Any food I can borrow?"

She turned to look at me. "It's almost bedtime and you haven't had supper? What happened?"

"If I start telling you the whole story without first getting some food, I'll probably drop dead before I get to the good part. I'm that hungry." She moved away from the corkboard wall and frowned. "Okay then, let's step into the kitchen and see what we can do?"

Dior's ears peaked at the word 'kitchen' and he beat us there.

I didn't even pretend to help. I sat at my favorite spot and waited. Within ten minutes a plate found its way in front of me. I don't know how she managed it, but a mouthwatering heap of steaming beef, carrots, mushrooms and water chestnuts covered a bed of rice. And, of course, a glass of Pinot Grigio. I knew she had smartly recycled some of the old pot roast we'd never gotten around to eating together, but I didn't care where all that goodness came from because I knew where it was headed. Ignoring Dior's well-rehearsed pleading look, I dug in.

ELEVEN

It was all coming back to me now, the reason I didn't like to drive anywhere before nine a.m. And yet, here I was, heading straight to the 32nd street entrance of the 51 South. All that because I couldn't think of any other way to get to Northern and Kassandra's condo. How crazy is that? Certainly there had to be another way. I blamed my directional brain fog on not getting enough sleep. It was pretty ironic that the loss of sleep was due not to the fear of what the future might bring but to the knowledge of what had already happened.

Sitting in Brenda's place, the evening before, eating her food and sharing a glass of wine had created the illusion of turning back time. To the way things were, better yet, the way *we* were. It only lasted the length of the meal. I would lie if I said that Brenda's confession that she was the one who told Sunny about Celine's stroll through the Psychic Fair didn't throw me for a loop.

How did Brenda know? Same way as Kassandra and the detectives, she told me. They all watched the same security camera footage. Sure enough, there was Celine buying something from the magic potions and lotions booth. Of course, after that reveal the elephant in the room was still Tristan's marital status. All Brenda shared was that while they were legally husband and wife, it was a marriage necessary for legal reasons. That's all she knew and, most important, all she felt free to share. She did stress that if it was so important to me I should ask Tristan directly. And on that sour note, I washed my plate, put it in the dishwasher and said good night. *Ask Tristan directly!* As if.

It seemed like my brain fog had been hanging around for a while, as I had a long list of unanswered texts, emails and, more urgent, phone calls. Today was the day, though. The minute I dropped Kassandra off at El Chorro to retrieve her Kia, I planned to make a beeline to the office, grab some coffee and sit in my cubicle until all those past due duties had been satisfied.

Oops, on the way to her condo I nearly bypassed the Northern exit. Apparently while the freeway was the busy place in the morning, traffic on Northern Avenue was flowing smoothly.

I crossed the main entrance of the Northern Star apartment complex and came to a screeching halt. Kassandra was waiting and ready to go. Good girl. I wondered how much she remembered about last evening.

"You may want to take Northern to Sixteenth Street and then south to Glendale Avenue," she said.

I bet she remembered everything.

I nodded and follow her suggestion. For a while neither of us spoke. Awkward.

"Now you know why," she said as I made a left on Glendale Avenue.

"Why what?"

"I normally don't drink hard stuff."

"Huh, that's why you got sooo, sooo..."

"So drunk? Yes, and you can say it. I don't get offended. I should have known better."

Mercy. I had nothing to say and willed myself to keep my eyes on the now snail-paced traffic and not look at Kassandra. She obviously felt remorseful enough she didn't need my two cents to top off the full glass of guilt.

We crossed over to the Paradise Valley side of the road without speaking. I had a million questions. Okay maybe not a million but at least a dozen. I checked her out sideways and she had nicely creased pants and a darling sweater I hadn't seen before. She had tamed her hair and exuded that nice, clean, fragrance of a fresh shower. The happy hour disaster would be our secret. Period.

That's what I told her. She patted my arm and whispered, "Thanks. I'll tell you what set me off when you're not driving." I sighed and kept my eyes on the road. We had just passed a Starbucks where cars lined up as if, instead of selling expensive, over-caffeinated brew, they were giving out free manna from the heavens. One of the most annoying American habits, in my opinion, was the rush to leave home early to get in line for some coffee. Seriously? For coffee? I once tried to explain the phenomenon to my mother who, by the way, never had a driver's license. She thought I was pulling her leg. *Pulling her leg*. Americanism in its purest form. Loved it. Try to translate that into Italian.

As anticipated, I beat Kassandra to the office. The front door was unlocked and I could smell coffee. I walked straight to the kitchen where I found Kay munching on some muffins. Blueberry I hoped. She had today's paper open in front of her but managed to slide the box with two more muffins my way. I went to get my mug and couldn't help notice that she was wearing the exact same clothes she had on yesterday. Interesting.

"Did you get my message?" Her voice spooked me, busy as I was mentally judging her assumed clothing faux pas.

"N-n-noo." Fingers crossed she wasn't a mind reader. I entertained myself removing the paper from the muffin. "That girl, the redhead. Her boss said she's good. She's covering for Al, that's why you ended up with her. You're one of Al's regulars. Anyway, the boss likes her. He plans to keep her on even after Al is back from his honeymoon. Let me see the photos when she sends them. You should be getting them today. I want to see just how good she is. Maybe I'll switch to her, too."

I mumbled okay, assembled my coffee and muffin, and headed to my cubicle. Hoped someone didn't take me for a trespasser, as I wasn't a familiar face around here before nine. But apparently Kay and I were the only early risers, or in her case, well, maybe she had yet to hit the sack. Oh, I should rephrase that. Later.

Kassandra arrived five minutes after I sat myself down at my desk. I waved at her from the cubicle. She headed to the kitchen and I could hear her talking and laughing, then the phones started to ring. I had four voicemails from Max. The last one must have come in just as I got into my Fiat. I checked the phone and sure enough, the ringer was off. Cool, Monica, really cool.

That's what professional realtors do, ignore their phones. I didn't recognize the number of the other two messages so, of course, I clicked on those first. Oh no, it was the assistant to the Esquire. I totally forgot about returning that call. Maybe it no longer mattered and they already settled without me. That would be a good thing, I told myself. Regardless, I had to call them. So that was the first message I returned, plus it counted for two.

The person at the other end sounded rather young and perky, for it being barely nine a.m., I mean.

"Oh, yes, Miss Baker, thank you for calling back. We would appreciate it if you could come by as soon as possible as everything must be signed and delivered by eleven o'clock." Eleven o'clock? It was after nine-thirty and I had no idea what she or her boss wanted me to sign.

So I asked her. There was a long pause before she answered. "Perhaps you would like to come in and review the documents? Should I let Mr. Dumont know you'll be stopping by so he can meet with you and go over everything?"

Just the mention of *his* name sent my blood scurrying all the way to my scalp. Great. I looked around. I was all alone. What a relief.

"Huh, no, no, that won't be necessary. If Mr. Dumont approved, it's all good. I'll be there within an hour, thanks."

I jotted down the address she gave me, same as on the fancy business card. It was in Scottsdale, not too far from my new listing. Perfect, I could swing by the Fashion Square Mall and pick up a few towels for the master bath. Within twenty minutes I was ready to hit the road, and had already explained to Kassandra and Kay. Two Ks, what a coincidence. The television jingle about every kiss begins with K stuck in my head like clumpy mascara on fake eyelashes for the rest of the morning.

The law firm office occupied the second floor of a building on the opposite side of the mall. The young lady in the lobby was the same one who answered my phone call. It all happened quickly. A beverage was offered, I declined. The documents were laid out on a huge, marble table in what could have been the conference room. A much older woman, a lawyer, greeted me and went over page after page of legalese. It all boiled down to the fact that I was about to get a $10,000 check as soon as everything was finalized. And that was for pain, suffering, stress and I didn't know what else. The lawyer assured me everything had Tristan Dumont's seal of approval and there was a strange gleam in her eyes when she pronounced his name. Almost like mentally letting me know she knew all about the two of us.

Stop it Monica. Yes, the same gleam the front desk girl had while walking me into the conference room. What? Did they think I was his mistress? Suddenly, I needed to get the hell out of there, go breathe some fresh air. I scribbled my name where the little yellow arrow pointed, no questions, no hesitation. I wanted to be done, wanted not to be there.

Then I rushed back to my car as if someone was chasing me. And I remembered I had, h-a-d, to get the car to the tire shop. So instead, I crossed the road and went shopping, hoping, praying, the hurt in my chest would subside. I picked up two large bath towels and two smaller ones, all white so I could use them for my own bath once the house sold. By then it was lunchtime so I stopped by the food court, something I hadn't done in a long time. Maybe by the time I was done with lunch I would no longer feel like calling Tristan. After all, thanks were in order.

I loved to eat and watch the crowd go by. You could tell the tourists by their short sleeves, shorts pants and some even in halter tops. Mercy. We locals wore sweaters, boots and even hoodies.

By one-thirty my phone let me know that R.E. Assist had sent a file to my work email. I could tell it was the file with the photos J.S. had taken. How exciting. Might as well run by the listing and find the best spot for the new towels. If all went as planned, I should post the home for sale by the next morning. Better hurry up. I wanted to give the sellers a chance to look over the photos before posting them. Oh yes, and show them to Kay, also, as promised. Plus she had to help me with the price. I already had the sellers' input. Shoot, always so many last minute details. And don't forget to check the tire. Seemed to hold up a lot better than me.

All I could think about was the best opening line for my call to Tristan. I started the engine and headed to the gated complex to place my new towels in the master bath.

TWELVE

I draped a newly purchased towel over the walk-in door of the bathtub. The tub itself appeared to have jets. Hmmm, do old people use that for relaxation or foreplay? Either way, who knew? Should I ask Brenda? Better have my running shoes on if I did that.

The mental image of Brenda's reaction made me smile. All that nonsense while being painfully aware of the day slipping away and the important real estate matters I had been neglecting. Time to step up my game, but first things first; use the bathroom. At that moment I sent mental thanks to Kay, who taught me to always leave a roll of toilet paper in your vacant listings. It brought good luck, she said.

Great advice.

I could swear I left a brand new roll in each bathroom when I was there for the photo shoot. But the one in the master had been used. And abused. How? I had the only key. Oh, wait. The sellers had keys. Oh, okay. They probably stopped by to make sure all was in fine order. Must call them, I promised to share the photos. I dried my hands on my jeans, locked everything up, and headed for my car. Something nagged at me, though I couldn't explain what. Before getting into the Fiat, I turned around to look at the lovely listing I had the good fortune to land. Fresh white paint and cute, just-for-show shutters on all the windows. Better recheck the doors I had already locked I decided. Enough, Monica. It's a gated community; their hired security do the rounds.

Ah, my tendency to see conspiracies everywhere. Brenda always blamed it on my bad habit of watching too many old Hitchcock movies.

Instead of using the main gate, I drove by the so-called country club and headed to the side gate. A quicker way to get back to Scottsdale Road. This entry gate only worked on remote, restricted to residents only. The exit, however, opened automatically. As I waited for the gate to open, someone was right on my tail. How annoying. Not my fault the darned gate moved slowly. Finally, I got out of the way and the small sports car zipped by me like its tail pipe was on fire. Probably someone's grandson, as the most popular vehicles around seemed to be golf carts. I was still swearing under my breath, *in Italian,* when I caught sight of a beat-up truck coming behind me on the passenger side. It made a sharp turn just before the exit gate closed on its rusty rear bumper. A gate crasher? What to do? What to do? Not much, I concluded. Who was I going to call? And say what?

Something about the camper seemed familiar. I kept on driving but the thought lingered that it might be the same one that tailed me yesterday.

Thirty minutes later I arrived at the Desert Homes Office parking lot. And not a minute too soon. I went straight to my computer and pulled up the file with the photos from the staging. Perhaps I looked flustered because Kassandra came by to ask me if I was okay.

"I'm good, but I think you should teach me how to read

Tarot cards. I could sure use the morning pick-me-up trick, like you do."

"It's not working," she said. "Wanna know why I drank too much the other evening? That ghost from the past I slept with keeps calling. Talks about leaving his wife and kids."

She shook her head in a disapproving way and walked back to her desk, not looking keen on my Tarot cards or the ghost from the past's brilliant ideas.

I have to say, J.S. did a great job considering all she had to work with was an empty house with outdated carpets and a few accent walls covered in wallpaper from way back before stainless steel appliances became so popular. As for the walk-in tub, there was no hiding that but maybe it would be a good selling point for the retired crowd. I immediately forwarded the complete package to Kay and the sellers. Playing catch-up had its advantage; it kept me focused, not letting my mind meander about Tristan's whereabouts. At some point I would need to call him, to thank him, to acknowledge the – gift? Settlement? Not sure what to call it... except money of course.

Kay's unmistakable laugh drifted up from her office. The doors must be open, meaning she was alone, a good time for me to go pick her brain, again.

She waved me in. I noticed the different outfit. So, she went home to change, like that was any of my business. My listing photos looked terrific on her computer screen. Kay agreed with me.

"Nice, the girl is a lousy reporter but a good photographer. I'll ask to be switched to her list. And I hear they are adding drone service for aerial views.

Our industry is changing by leaps and bounds but I'm not going to do the drone unless the listing is over 500K. By the way, is your aunt still booking catering jobs for December or is she full?"

"I will have to check on that." I said.

Suddenly last night's sight of Brenda's house ablaze in lights and then her standing in the center of her pantry deep in thought. What was that all about? I never even asked. I only cared about my stomach... and my heart.

Today was Tuesday. I counted on my fingers and figured out the house with the tub would be officially for sale to the public by Thursday morning. Time to get the realty sign up. I could go by tomorrow to install the lock box in case some interested party kept an eye on the subdivision. We would be the only active listing. Whoo hooo, no competition. And then I remembered Scott, somewhere in Utah, skiing. Damn. And the tire — had to take care of that. The last thing I needed was another flat tire on the way to meet a client.

I pulled out my monthly planner and called my mechanic. He could have the tire in the shop by morning and I would need to sit and wait for about forty-five minutes. Forty-five minutes in mechanic speak meant about double that. I sighed. Made a note, car/tire, 9:30. And then I made the mistake of looking at the actual date. An alarm went off in the pit of my stomach. I was late, really late.

I'd been subconsciously blocking it off. And that was probably the main reason I didn't want to listen to Max's messages. The thought made me crazy. How could it even be possible? I had never been one to take chances on that subject. No siree, never. The angst at the pit of my stomach had a name: unplanned pregnancy? I felt sick, no not the morning sickness, the other kind that gets you when you're faced with the possibility of being a complete irresponsible fool, one who's probably ruined your life forever.

Breathe, Monica, breathe. I didn't even know how many days one had to wait before rolling the dice on a store-bought kit. Would check on that with my home computer. The quiet of the office, so unusual, crept under my skin. Anxiety and anger grew. I had to do something before I exploded. I walked up to Kassandra's desk. She was engrossed in the latest issue of People magazine. Talk about a slow day at the office.

"Where is everybody? I haven't seen Sunny in two days. And what about Scott? I need the sign installed. Did you see the photos? That's J.S.'s work. I think she did a good job. Kay is going to start using her also." I spit all that out without coming up for air.

Kassandra listened, her eyes on me, not blinking. She closed the magazine slowly and laid it on her desk. Then she tilted her head and seemed to study me. For a very long time. "What the hell happened to you? If you need to talk to Sunny I'm sure you know how to use a phone. If you need a post installed, it would be a good idea to fill out a request form or do you think you're so special that Scott can just read your mind? You know what? I think I do need to read your cards, but not while you look at me with crazed eyes."

Lucky for me she spoke without raising her voice. I was this close to start crying. How was that for all-grown-up Monica Baker? And just like that, puff, all my anger dissipated and I ran into the kitchen and blew my nose and caught a wandering tear before it ever had a chance to roll off the slippery slope of my sad face. Time for me to go home.

I made it as far as the parking lot and sat in the car, bargaining with myself and with God. The last time I did that was when my grandmother was in the hospital. My bargaining didn't work then, would probably not work now. Time to *bite the bullet*, or in this case buy the pregnancy kit. Dear God. The idea of doing that made me want to die. I would have to find a drug store, not close to home, with a woman cashier, about my age. Sooo embarrassing. Pay cash so it couldn't be traced back to me. My cell interrupted my important scheming project. "Are you still sitting in your pink can in the parking lot?"

Kassandra. Could she see me from her desk? Shit. I started the engine.

"Was." Could only manage a word before choking up.

"How about you come back in here and tell me what's going on? And don't start on the Tarot cards. That's for b-e-f-o-r-e, not after."

"You know about it? How? I haven't told anyone. Hell, I'm not even sure myself."

Silence.

"I meant you get a reading when you're seeking help on making a decision, a choice. Stop acting like a dumb ass and come tell me what's going on. I'm closing up as soon as Kay leaves. But I can't run out there."

My car inched toward the main road. "I am, no, *I think*, I may be pregnant."

"And?" Did she say 'And?' What was wrong with her?

"I need to find out." I whispered.

"Speak up, I can hardly hear you."

"I don't know for sure."

"Let me guess, you're what? Five, ten minutes past the time you think you should start menstruating and you are coming unglued. I'm sure if you were over twenty-four hours late you would have already done your pee test, right?"

I didn't know what to say. Part of me felt offended, but the wiser part knew she was on target, and she was a friend.

"No, I've been debating where to buy one of those things, you know, the pregnancy kit like they show on TV?"

"Well girl, this is your lucky day, debate no more. If you can wait until morning I'll bring you one and you can satisfy your curiosity."

"No, no, I don't mean for you to go buy... oh, I could pay you back. But at the office? How?"

"I keep a half dozen in my fridge at home. It's cheaper buying in bulk."

I couldn't tell if she was being funny to cheer me up or if... after all, this was Kassandra I was talking to.

"You just show up and I'll walk you through it. Now go home and get drunk because if you are and... never mind. The phone is ringing. Do as I said."

I was stunned. A car to my right honking urgently snapped me back to reality in a jiffy. My Fiat was half on the main street and half on the sidewalk. Way to go, Monica. I instinctively straightened out the car and headed home. Had to get myself together in case I ran into Brenda, or worse yet, Brenda and Bob. Brenda and Bob. B&B. Like the name of *our* catering company. How about that? She could easily kick me out and have Bob as a business partner and...

What was I thinking? Enough nonsense for one day! My cell chimed again and I was oh, so tempted to roll down the window and toss the phone. I didn't.

"Hello, Monica, is this a good time to talk?" J.S. Smith.

"Huuuh? I — yes." I swallowed hard, "Sure, I'm driving and I'm alone, go ahead. What's up? Oh, by the way, very nice job with the pics."

"You're too kind. That's sort of why I'm calling. My manager told me that one of the top high-end agents asked to use my services based on the photos I did for you."

"You mean Kay. Yes, she's in my office and yes, she sells high-priced properties. Maybe you don't remember her, but she was at that open house where we met for the first time."

She sighed. "Hope she doesn't remember me. I was working for that gossip magazine and making a pest of myself. Anyway, I created some color fliers for your listing. They turned out pretty good, and I also put together a folder with all the photos for your sellers to keep. Can I come by your office first thing in the morning and show you?"

I'm not good at driving and talking; I tend to slow down to snail pace to the extreme annoyance of all the other drivers behind me. I was collecting a nice sample of hateful looks and a few finger signals. "I have to take my car in to get a new tire at 9:30 and will probably be sitting and waiting for an hour or so."

"How about if I come and rescue you from the waiting room, we run over to your listing, set up the little display I made and I'll drive you back. You won't get bored and I'll feel great for helping you out."

I turned left, taking the back road that ran by Tristan's house. Just how sick-minded was I?

"Sounds terrific, Jessie, as soon as I get home I'll text you the address and phone number of my mechanic. Perfect timing, too, I'll put on the lock box. We are releasing the listing Thursday morning."

The Dumont home was dark except for the outdoor low-voltage lights, probably solar. I couldn't call Tristan after business hours; it would be too personal. Plus it might annoy his wife if they were having dinner together. My mind went wondering about the kind of food they would eat. Who did the cooking? Lois Thomas, Angelique's personal assistant? And how was that any of my business? I had more serious problems to tackle.

I finally left 36th street and started to relax, until I arrived in view of home. I noticed Bob Clarke's car first. Blocking the driveway. My driveway. Okay, shared driveway, but still. Wait... was that Tommy's Harley? What the hell was going on? My ex and Officer Clarke? Who else? Was this a family party minus me?

I parked my car on the street, as close as possible to the sidewalk, and caught a glimpse of the widow across the street peeking from behind her drapes. I had barely locked my car door when Dior came barreling down the driveway and nearly knocked me off my feet. If

Dior was loose, something must have happened to Aunt Brenda. I grabbed the Great Dane's collar and marched up to the house.

THIRTEEN

"Slow down," meant nothing to Dior. We flew up the concrete driveway to the open back door of Brenda's place. Wide open, same as the garage door. I recognized two of Brenda's dining chairs sitting outside, by the garage. Her Honda Pilot parked as far in as possible and the rear door of the SUV also wide open. Voices could be heard inside the home. Well, voices, clatter, grinding noises, a cacophony of sounds I had a hard time identifying, except for Brenda's raspy laugh, trademark of lifelong smokers. I had so missed that laugh.

What was happening? Was someone moving? Moving in or out? A sense of panic found its way down my chest where angst and fear had been doing the tango ever since I discovered that I was late with my period. I doubted anyone knew of my presence until Dior let out a rather assertive series of barks. The Great Dane had a knack for gathering an audience in a split second.

Tommy and his curly black hair materialized first. Peeking out from the open door.

"Oh, it's you," he said. "Wait." He called out, "Aunt Brenda, your dog is here in back, with Monica."

"What? How did he get out?" Brenda called.

The automatic security lights came on as I stood there, mouth open, holding Dior's collar until Brenda appeared.

"Oh, hi Monica, I didn't hear your car. Where did you find that bad boy?"

Brenda was still talking when Bob appeared behind her. In jeans and a flannel shirt with the sleeves rolled up, he looked hot and his wide forehead shone with perspiration, but he was smiling.

I couldn't think of a thing to say, so I just did a little balancing dance from one foot to the other and waited.

"We're making room for the home gym, but some of my stuff will have to go." Brenda walked over and got hold of the Dane.

"The home what?" I gasped.

I could feel Tommy's eyes on me and it made me extremely uncomfortable, but I wasn't sure why.

"Gym, gym." Brenda laughed again and it occurred to me this was the first time since the 'incident' that I had seen her so happy and relaxed. And in spite of her nephew's presence. Incredible.

"I have some chicken breasts in the oven. Nothing fancy because we need to get this done tonight. You're welcome to join us." She waited for my answer.

I looked from Bob to Tommy and my response was clear. "Huh, that's okay, I have paperwork to do. I'm taking my car in in the morning for the tire. So, thanks. You three go ahead, get your gym done."

Bob had already disappeared into the house and I could hear furniture being moved, scraping the floor.

"I tell you what, I'll send Tommy over with some dinner when it's done. OK? Wait, where is your car?"

"On the street. I'll get it later." I turned around and headed to my own place. I couldn't stand Tommy's stares. They made me feel self-conscious, like he knew something about me that he wasn't supposed to. Yes, I had gone completely bonkers.

In spite of all my good intentions, I ended up changing into sweats and Googling all kinds of idiotic scenarios regarding unplanned pregnancies and false alarms. My stomach growled, but now that Brenda had offered me some of her chicken, nothing taking up room in my fridge looked appetizing. And just then, a light knocking at the door. I slipped on my chunky hiking shoes, because I was familiar with Tommy's dirty tricks.

I opened the door, barely ajar, and promptly placed my foot on the threshold where I knew he would try to insert his to keep me from closing the door. He held a plate in his hand and an ambiguous smile in his dark eyes. "Aren't you going to ask me in?"

"No. I'm sure Brenda and Bob need you there."

I grabbed the edge of the warm plate and he pulled back.

"Okay then, have it your way."

I moved back and put my weight against the door, aware if he really wanted to force his way in, I didn't stand a chance. Tommy may have been rotten, but he wasn't totally stupid. He handed me the dish.

"By the way, I'll be moving in next door, to help Aunt Brenda get the gym set up."

And on those words of forthcoming doom, he left. Good riddance, for now. The idea of my ex moving in, even if temporarily, messed up my appetite. But nothing a glass of wine couldn't fix. The quiet of my place felt spooky. So my chewing the fabulous chicken swimming in a mild cheesy sauce surrounded by potatoes and broccoli must have sounded like a Great Dane ripping apart a large bone.

Between being late, knowing that my abusive, former husband was spending the night a few yards from my bed, and having to choose between leaving my car parked on the road overnight or go ask Bob to move his car and chance having Tommy tailing me to the Fiat, well, I didn't have enough wine in the fridge to improve my mood.

I turned on the television and watched a rerun of Two Broke Girls even though I didn't like the show or the way they portrayed working women. I ate every little bite of my dinner, skipped dessert and sent a mental goodnight to my poor Fiat 500 sitting alone in the cold Phoenix night. After rinsing the dish and the silverware, I filled my stem glass with ice cubes and water, turned off the television and the lights, tucked myself into bed in my sweats and cried myself to sleep.

Morning light found me in the same *why me* kind of attitude that had lulled me to sleep. As I brushed my teeth I remembered Kay and her catering question. I never mentioned it to Brenda just as I had never listened to any of Max's voice mails. I hated myself. Love or hate, I needed to look the part. I wore a skirt, boots, and a sweater with matching cardigan, what I called my old lady outfit. With everything I would need for the day neatly packed in the briefcase Brenda gave me two Christmases ago.

Trying not to alert Dior of my presence, I tiptoed out of the house and down the driveway to my lonely pink beauty with the long scratch left by Celine's key as obvious as a battle scar in the early sunlight. The seat cover felt cold against my bare legs. Note to myself, wear longer skirts on winter mornings. After all, it was a frigid 60 degrees out here. I made it to the mechanic with ten minutes to spare. And my new tire had yet to be delivered. Great.

I poured myself a cup of Mark the mechanic's awful, strong coffee, texted Brenda about Kay's catering question, and while I debated calling Max, J.S. arrived all bubbly and cheerful. I let Mark know about my quick escape to the new listing and he promised to keep me posted via texting.

J.S. drove the R.E. Assist small van. I liked the way the seats were higher than normal cars and I had a better view of the road and surroundings. An empty Starbucks container sat in the cup holder of the center console. "I have the sellers' folder and the fliers in the back seat," She said. "Are you excited?"

I nodded. "There is something different about this listing," I said. "I'm not sure how to explain. Maybe because of the age of the home and the sense of nostalgia it projects."

"Or maybe it's that walk-in tub," she chided. None of us mentioned Tristan Dumont, but the air in the van was filled with the vibes of amber eyes.

When we arrived at the house, she punched in the numbers I called out and the big metal gate opened with a low groan.

"Well, I expected more activity on the streets," I said. "Aren't old folks supposed to be early risers?"

"It's after nine," she laughed. "Probably almost nap time."

A truck with a landscape logo sat askew by the side of the road, a few men were busy raking, and others made a racket with a leaf blower. By the time we reached the house, we left the din behind. I felt invigorated, maybe because of J.S.'s bubbly energy permeating the van or maybe because with all the green around and the small man-made lake in the distance, it felt more like a day in the country than work.

"Let me try the duplicate key I had made for the lock box," I said, "and then I'll let you in."

J.S. was scanning the view, unconcerned. "No hurry, I only have a twilight shoot this evening, way on the other side of town. My time is your time."

I had to admit, she had a pretty good attitude in spite of our rough beginning way back when J.S. wrote a scandalous piece about Tristan and Celine. They'd been considered an item, at least by some of us. Having been one of those people and having the scar on the Fiat to prove it. Celine's pay back.

The duplicate worked fine. I dropped it in the lockbox, attached it to the outside water faucet and kept the original key in my purse. I opened the door, moved aside and let J.S. in first. She headed for the kitchen.

"We could set up the display with the fliers and the other printouts I made with general information of the area on the kitchen counter, easily visible from the entrance."

"Sounds good to me."

I went to open the kitchen mini blinds. A large, dried up brown spot covered part of the bottom of the white sink. "What happened here?" I yelled.

J.S walked over. "What is it?" She ran a finger over the stain.

"Watch it," I cautioned. "What if it's some kind of chemical?"

She sniffed her finger, shrugged. "Are you always that cautious? It's soda, dried up Pepsi or something similar. Can't tell. All the colas smell the same."

I could feel my face screwing up into a frown. I didn't like this. "How did it get there? I checked the whole house yesterday. The sink was clean."

"You're sure? Little things like that are easy to miss." She turned on the water, "Here." The brown spot disappeared along with the water. And J.S. went back to her display setting while I walked around the house, checking every nook and cranny and every shower, every sink, every whatever.

Paranoia, my steady companion. The dreadful sense of someone else having been in the house followed me from room to room.

"Still concerned about the sink?" J.S. was all smiles. Perhaps S stood for Sunshine. "Come see."

I followed her back into the kitchen where her display was already set up and it looked very professional. Prospective buyers and realtors alike would be impressed by my presentation, even if I was a newbie.

"A newbie with talented friends." I hugged her. "Thank you so much. The mechanic hasn't called yet. Want to look at the walk in tub? The yard?"

She tilted her head back and forth, her raven curls bobbing along her shoulders while she considered my offer. "We could do that or we could go grab a bite to eat at the restaurant close to here. I hear they have a nice yet modestly priced buffet."

A girl after my own heart. A food lover. "Good idea, my treat. I insist. We can cut through the back and walk there. And you know what? I'll leave one of the windows open to get some air circulating. I can't stand those flowery plug-ins."

"What are we waiting for?" She grabbed her purse and after locking the front door from inside, we left thorough the back door.

We had just finished eating our eggs and hash browns when my phone chimed. My car was ready to be picked up. As if on cue, we both grabbed a muffin, wrapped it in a paper napkin, and after I left a few dollars tip on the table, we rushed out.

"I feel like we are playing hooky," she giggled.

"You too? This has been fun. I need to go in and lock up the window I left open."

"Okay, you do that and I'll get the van started."

We went into the house the same way we left but I turned left to go lock the window, and she turned right to go out front door to her vehicle.

"Hey, hey you, get away from that van." I heard her scream before I even reached the open window. I turned around, accidently dropped my keys, but kept on running to help J.S.

FOURTEEN

My rescue run came to a screeching halt when I caught a glimpse of J.S.

Hands on hips and seemingly very confrontational, she looked and acted pretty much in-your-face to some man standing a whole head taller than she was. What the hell? They had to know each other. Either that or 'private space' meant to them as much as 'no more husbands' had meant to Elizabeth Taylor after hubby #2.

I tried hard to eavesdrop from a distance, gave up and inched a bit ahead, you know, in case J.S. needed my, ahem, assistance.

"What's going on?" That's all I got to say before J.S. turned her head and blocked me with a forceful, "I got this."

And believe me, I was instantly convinced. Ouch. Something in her voice and body language seemed pricklier than a Hindu bed of nails. I didn't walk away nor did I move closer. I watched in fascination as the 'war dance' of those two proceeded. For every forward step J.S. took, the man moved one back. I still couldn't get a good view of the trespasser; he was partly hidden by the van. And then there was Miss 'I stand my ground' smack in front of him.

Even with her voice on a rising scale, I couldn't understand a word they said. She stopped talking, and in a sudden 180 degree move, he turned around and walked away. Neither J.S. nor I stirred. Then the strangest thing happened. The man's pace slowed and he turned his head to look squarely at J.S. and my heart stopped. That was the man who had followed me the day I was driving Kassandra's Kia. The man with the muddy, rusty camper. OMG!!! Breathe Monica, breathe.

J.S. walked over to where I stood petrified. "Ready to go? Did you lock up?" Cool as wet sand at low tide.

I shook my head no. Even with my mouth wide open I couldn't find a word to say. Finally I gulped air and headed back to the house to get the keys and lock it up. The whole time still searching for a smart question for this suddenly alien, redheaded woman.

We went from camaraderie to awkward in less time than it takes to read the 140 characters of a tweet.

I sat on the passenger seat, stiff as a dried up marshmallow. We didn't speak until we reached Scottsdale Road. "What was that all about?" I asked with as much assertiveness I could fake.

She let out a long, long sigh, so long and soft it sounded like a mourning cry. And I watched her body relax, a balloon doll after they let the air out. "That — was my father."

Wham! What was that she said? "Your — fath — father?"

"Estranged father." Her voice grew stronger. "Haven't seen him in maybe five, six years."

"And he knew you worked for R.E. Assist?"

"I didn't ask, although I doubt it. He was probably looking to break into the van and steal whatever he could grab."

"Wow. Do you know where he lives?"

She shook her head no.

"I ask because," I cleared my throat. Mercy this was hard, "Because I think he's the man who cut me off yesterday, on Camelback Road. I was driving Kassandra's Kia and, okay, it was partly my fault, anyway he was in a beat up camper, got me all scared. But then he stopped me and simply suggested I pay more attention to my driving, and I can't say he was totally wrong."

She didn't answer, just watched me with a sideways glance.

"What is he doing here? You think he followed us? Oh, no, I mean, where was his camper?"

As I said that, the camper with the rusty bumper crashing the gate yesterday flashed through my mind. And the hair on the back of my neck stood to attention.

"He said he has a job as a groundskeeper. I've never known him to tell the truth." She spoke softly, uncomfortably.

The sight of Mark's auto repair place made me feel like singing. I thanked J.S. We even hugged briefly and I got out of her van so fast a passerby may have assumed I was escaping a snatching gone wrong.

That creep was her father.

Holly crap! Gave all new meaning to dysfunctional family.

After paying for my new tire, I drove to the office in a mental fog. And found the parking lot nearly full. What had happened? Did I miss some memo about a party? Realtors hardly ever miss something fun and free. Well at least I wore real business clothes. Bring it on. I made it all the way to the doorstep, had my hand on the door handle when I remembered my cell. Left it on the car seat. Needed the phone. I quickly headed back to my Fiat and saw him.

Max. Standing, no, leaning against my car, waiting. Where did he come from? And the dark cloud I managed to push aside all day crashed on me with all its might. Did he know? How?

We faced each other for an awkward moment. No words, no embraces. Silence.

He spoke first. "Hi, Monica." The voice of a polite stranger. The unanswered phone calls and messages from him clearly flashing in my mind.

"Well, what a surprise." I attempted a smile. "When did you get back?"

"What do you care?"

Ouch.

"I'm just here a few days. I sold my karate studio. We are closing the deal tomorrow."

I opened my mouth to ask how that came to be and stopped. He undoubtedly told me all about it in his messages and tried to reach me many times to tell me personally. Well done, Monica.

His incredible blue eyes looked more doll-like today than ever before because, besides being such an intense color, they were also as cold and unemotional as plastic eyes. I had it coming. From the man who may be the father of my unborn child.

"Came to say goodbye. I'm moving to Colorado. I met someone." His eyes a mere slit. "She loves me, always answers my calls." He sneered. "Not that you would care, but I wanted you to hear it from me."

I was still gulping air and only managed to say, "You've always been the better person."

A smile lit his face, a smile of great satisfaction that meant, "I know."

He tapped me lightly on the shoulder, moved away from my car, and I watched him get into a bronze-colored Jeep Cherokee with a ski rack on the roof and drive out of the parking lot and out of my life.

I had to sit; my legs felt like twigs in the wind. Winds of change. I hid in my pink car, closed the door, rested my head on the steering wheel and cried. A loud engine snapped me out of my self-pity party. A truck parked next to me. Scott's truck. Was he already back from the skiing trip? I looked into the rearview mirror and quickly wiped my cheeks with the back of my hands. Where is a tissue when you need one? And there was Scott, knocking on my car window.

"Hey Monica, I just installed your sign. Nice listing. I put a rider on the post, with your cell number. Did you just get here or are you leaving?"

He removed other agents' sign riders from the back of his truck.

That was my cue. Got out of my car and followed Scott into the office. "Why so many vehicles?" I asked.

"Celine." He snorted, "She's doing some girls crap. I don't know. Ask Kassandra."

The last person I wanted to see was Celine. Oh well, maybe she did her thing in her mother's office. I hurried to keep up with Scott's long, fast strides. "What happened to your ski trip?"

"I skied one afternoon, cost me about $100 and I nearly froze my butt off. So I turned around and came back. I'll go up to Flagstaff on Saturday. I hear they have a few inches of fresh powder."

I nodded, "Snowbowl?"

"Yeah, wanna join me?"

Like a weekend with a young dude and his beer guzzling buddies was on my playlist. "Huh, no. Hate snow," I mumbled as he opened the door to the office and let me in.

Kassandra barely acknowledged our presence. She seemed peeved somehow. Scott took a look around, about half dozen females in their twenties were taking up space here and there, while Celine, all dressed in Christmassy colors, moved around with a basket filled with I don't know what.

Scott dropped the riders on Kassandra's desk, then pivoted on his heels saying, "I'm out of here." Loud. Then under his breath, "Bitches."

True Scott. At least he made Kassandra smile.

"Is it safe to go to my desk?" I asked.

"Hey, there was a hottie with a tight ass looking for you. You just missed him."

I shook my head, remembering Max. "No, I didn't."

"Oh, oh. Is that? That's him. Right? Why are you so grouchy about it? I got your... emergency kit... but I suggest you wait until the swarm of wannabees leaves."

"What are they doing?"

She shrugged, "Maids of honor to someone's wedding? All Celine's girlfriends. Was supposed to happen at Sunny's place, but something about tree roots and backed up sewers changed their plans. So they ended up here. And the brainless blonde gives me a list and expects me to have food and booze delivered. As if. Freaking B**H. She's going around with that stupid basket and they pick the names of who's doing what. So, you going out with your hot stud? Did you tell him?"

"Tell him what? And no, he came by to let me know he's moving to Colorado where he found true love."

Why did I say that? I couldn't stand the look of *oh, you poor girl* I was getting from Kassandra.

"I'm going home."

I left as fast as I could so she wouldn't have a chance to make me change my mind. And without the pregnancy kit she'd promised me.

I'm not going to cry. I'm not going to cry. It had been that kind of day. My cell chimed.

"Hey," I sighed. "Hi, Brenda."

"Please, curb your enthusiasm," she chided.

"You're speaking television sitcom now?"

"I couldn't resist. What's wrong?" she asked and it felt awkward. For weeks she'd been the one who was depressed and withdrawn. Now that she seemed to have bounced back, my life was coming unraveled. "Oh, you know. This and that."

"This and that? How do you come up with those answers? Is it work?"

I felt like a real jerk. "Sorry. No, and by the way, thanks for getting me that listing. It goes on the market in the morning." Now that I had her attention, I had to ask her a question I'd been avoiding. "Brenda, are you giving up the catering business?"

"Give up my catering? Of course not. But I'm making changes. Trying to create a more 'healthy' image. That's the reason for the home gym. I'll be part of the healthy image, right?"

"Right."

"I'm running late and I was wondering if you can check on Dior."

"Is Tommy at your house?"

"That's just it. I don't know. He was supposed to get the setup completed today and take the dog for a walk. But he isn't answering the phone and I'm a little concerned. If you get home before I do, could you take care of Dior for me?"

"I'm two minutes from home. I'll take Dior for a walk, I can use some exercise anyway. I just don't like to be around your nephew, sorry."

"Totally justified. He's going back to his place this evening and Bob is working the late shift. Why don't you plan on coming over and I'll tell you about the new project?"

"The new project? With Officer Clarke?" My sarcasm couldn't be missed.

"Of course not. He isn't getting involved with the actual day-to-day business. Hey, got to run. See you in a few hours and don't let Tommy get to you."

I drove into my own garage. No sign of Tommy or his motorcycle. Didn't know if that was good or bad. I went inside, changed from my business clothes to sweats and sneakers. With phone and keys in my pocket, I knocked on Brenda's back door. As soon as he heard me, Dior began barking and scratching. I counted to ten and then let myself in with the extra key. Inside, the house was dark. Dior jumped on me and before I made it past the kitchen, I knew he had pooped somewhere in the house. The stink was overwhelming. Damn.

"Tommy," I called out. "Anyone?" No answer.

I started to walk around, opening drapes and blinds, stepping carefully. The house was a mess. It looked like whoever had been assembling what looked like a treadmill had quit before finishing the job. Open cardboard boxes, screwdrivers and I didn't know what else lay scattered everywhere. Dior didn't look too happy either.

Could he have been locked in the house all day? I walked into the kitchen and sure enough, I found an empty water bowl and no food. No wonder the poor boy whined. I fed him, gave him water, scratched his head and then followed my nose.

He had relieved himself as close to the door between the laundry room and the garage as possible. Poor thing. At least he did it on the tile. In five minutes I had cleaned up and packed the mess in plastic bags. As soon as he was finished eating, I put his leash around his neck and we left for a long walk. Couldn't wait to see Brenda's reaction when she got home. Yep, as always, Tommy was true to himself.

FIFTEEN

Like a child set free after hours of sitting in a boring classroom, Dior could hardly contain his excitement. He moved fast, forcing me to trot after him. We headed toward Shea Boulevard and passed by neighbor Bob's house. Not to be confused with Officer Robert Clarke, Bob to his friends. High on a ladder, neighbor Bob busied himself untangling Christmas lights.

"Hey Monica, what's going on at your place?"

I slowed down in spite of Dior's impatience.

"I don't know. Why don't you tell me? By the time I usually get home, this whole street is either sleeping or watching TV."

"I'm talking about late morning, noon maybe?"

"Sheesh, I left early, had to get new tires. Brenda was home. Oh, Tommy, my ex is helping his aunt set up some exercising equipment. Was he making a lot of noise? Banging, drilling?"

I couldn't see Bob's expression with him up by the roof and me on the sidewalk, but I could hear him laughing. "Banging and drilling sounds about right. Until the shouting and screaming started. After that Tommy flew by on his Harley. I could swear he was shoeless and had the little two-seater sports car right on his ass. That Tommy, same skirt chaser. Oh, sorry, Monica, didn't mean to – you know..."

"No apologies needed, we're divorced, remember? Better get going, I promised Dior a long walk and it's getting dark."

I left in a hurry before he felt like spilling more details I'd rather not know about. However, that sort of explained the state of disarray in Brenda's house. Had Tommy actually brought a woman there? None of my business. It felt so good not being married to him I found myself skipping while Dior pulled me toward 40th street.

It didn't take long for my wandering mind to think of Tommy and Max. They had nothing in common and yet I didn't manage to play nice with either.

I might be pregnant by the one who might have made a good partner. Maybe... maybe... I was the problem, not *them*. Me. And on that happy thought I found myself at the intersection of 40th street and Shea. The Great Dane knew the way to the mountain preserve better than a trained hound. Might as well go to the end, take a little jog and get back home. Plenty of streets lights and paved roads for an easy, safe stroll. It had been a while since I hiked the trails, and, maybe because of winter, even the parking lot at the trailhead felt a little spooky. To me I mean, not to crazy, happy Dior. He pulled on that leash like a freight train.

"Okay, boy, calm down, we are not going up the trail, it's too late."

We jogged around the circular parking lot that still had some vehicles, and of course I'd forgotten my water bottle. I headed toward the public drinking fountain in case Dior was thirsty, too. After all, I had no idea how long his water bowl had been dry. Maybe all day. And I also forgot to let Brenda know we went for a walk.

Damn. What if she got home and saw the house all messed up and her dog missing? Better call her. I moved closer to the public bathrooms so I could see what I was dialing. Before I even touched the screen, Dior leaped ahead, pulling me along. What the hell? What spooked him?

"Will you stop acting like a fool? Dior. Stop it," I called to no avail.

I held tightly on the leash and he barked. What got him so riled up? I looked around, a car engine running, two hikers coming down from the number 8 trail, and a horse and rider approaching the parking lot from trail 100. The Great Dane was barking at the horse rider. And me? I mentally prayed for the ground to open and swallow me, but, please, spare Dior as he had nothing to do with my emotional shortcomings.

"Fiat? Is that you?" Tristan's words seemed synchronized with the clippety-clop of the Appaloosa's hooves. *Is that why I came here? Hoping to run into him?* If that was the case why was I wearing old sweats with a stretched-out bottom and why did I not put on at least a smudge of lipstick? Needed to have a serious talk with my subconscious.

Now Dior was in full performance mode, jumping and barking and running around me, hitting my legs with his powerful tail. You'd think he was having a full-blown affair with the mare. Could my secret wants be contagious? Could I be more idiotic than this? While my brain churned scenarios by a Baker's dozen, my body didn't budge, not even one iota. The day's dramas, doubts and dreams stayed neatly stacked inside my chest, behind the faded fleece hoodie. Tristan dismounted his horse and walked her up to where I was trying to restrain my dog gone wild. It felt like déjà vu. He wore the same clothes and boots he had on the first time I ran into him on the trail, except for a denim jacket over the white shirt and minus the red bandana.

Tache, the appaloosa, lowered her head to sniff the dog. How about that? Shouldn't it be the other way around? Dusk wiped away the last traces of daylight, and I wished I could do the same with the disturbing thoughts galloping through my mind.

"They like each other." Tristan pointed to the Dane and the horse sniffing and checking each other out. "Such an unexpected and pleasant surprise to run into you two."

If voices were like cupcakes, his would be red velvet with butterscotch frosting. Yum. He was so close I could see his Adam apple and the amber specs dancing in his eyes. *I must say something*. "Yeah, well, it's getting late, I need to head back." *Brava* Monica, *bravissima*. What a great line. Even in the looming darkness his pained smile was hard to miss. I hated, *hated* myself for it. He had been so nice to me, not like Tommy, or Max. Well, better leave Max out of the comparison, at least for now. After all, this was not a competition.

"You're right," he said. "It's getting late. Let me walk you down to Shea where there are more lights and people. I would offer to escort you home but guiding a horse on a main street in the dark is not a good idea. Some drivers are too busy texting or worse." He paused. "Is that okay with you?"

"Huh, okay. What?"

He cocked his head and smiled. "Oh, girl, what am I going to do with you?" And he laughed, an open, friendly laugh.

I returned a smile and tugged on the leash. "Let's go Dior, these good souls are guiding us back to civilization." Everything was going to be okay.

Tristan laughed again, this time softly, took my hand, intertwined his fingers with mine, sending electrifying waves up my spine. We walked out of the nearly deserted parking lot, Tristan holding his horse reins, while I dragged a disappointed dog.

We headed toward Shea Boulevard, because the only other way was to the dark mountain.

"Fiat," he said slowly, "I understand your feeling uncomfortable being too friendly with me. And I respect your strong work ethic."

My strong work ethic? Was he poking fun at me?

"Soon the Horse Ranch escrow will close and you'll no longer be my agent, which in this case, makes me very happy as I would like for us to be more than that."

I could see the light at the intersection turn red, a good thing because he couldn't see the crimson tide overtaking my cheeks.

"More than what? Aren't we forgetting a small detail?" Keep moving, Monica. Don't stop. Don't look at him.

Keep walking.

I quickened my pace, felt his fingers slowly slip away, letting go of my hand. He took my elbow instead and forced me to stop. The light went from red to green. We were feet from reaching the main road. Soon he would turn around, walk his horse home. Please let me go. I can't handle more heartache, not today.

"A small detail? Can you be more specific?" No more butterscotch frosting.

"You're a married man." The words hung in the night air now, turning amber-colored, like his eyes, like the traffic signal. Stop!

He stepped squarely in front of me, still holding Tache's reins. The shift confused Dior, who moved back a bit. Tristan, a head taller than me, bent a little, getting closer. Perhaps trying to look into my eyes? Tache snorted impatiently.

"I explained all that to you in my message."

The *message*. I bit my lips hard. Some things you don't forget. The memory of the messages appearing next to each other on my phone. Tristan's and Max's. My heart yearned for Tristan's, my conscience settled on Max's. And Tristan's message was deleted, unread, to avoid further temptation.

"Remember? After you visited me, when I was bedridden?"

I couldn't look at him. Even in this changing light I recognized the hurt mantling the face I so adored.

"I wanted everything out in the open between us." Hurt and disappointment threaded through his words.

I lowered my eyes. He straightened up, tall and proud again. Stepped back next to his mare. "You never read it, did you? You never cared to." A whisper. And he was gone.

The light turned green. I crossed the street on the marked walk and let the tears free fall.

Trifecta, I repeated furiously, pulling Dior along. Tommy, Max, Tristan. Trifecta. The screeching of brakes snapped me out of my self-imposed slide to hell.

"What are you two night owls doing on the streets so late?"

Brenda!

"Hop in."

And hop in, we did. As usual Dior sat in the back for all of twenty seconds. The minute the Honda moved, he crept forward and soon his snout rested on the center console. Both Brenda and I pretended not to notice. Dior, our lovable, invisible Dane.

"Where have you two been?" she asked.

"I took Dior for a walk. I don't think he had been let out all day. I cleaned up and gave him food and water, and really you can't blame the dog."

"What are you saying?" By her side glances I knew she was trying to read my thoughts. If only she could.

"I'm saying Tommy must have left the house in the morning and didn't come back, at all."

"Don't tell me. I bet he never finished setting up the equipment." Again, glancing at me.

"I'm not getting involved. It's between you two. I felt sorry for poor Dior."

"Just how sorry did you feel? I can tell you've been crying. Did that son of a..." (she swore so ladylike it sounded like B***H) "do something to you? I swear I'll kill him."

"No, Brenda. Haven't seen Tommy at all. Relax."

“So, why the crying?”

“It’s — hormonal — you know.”

I shut up, tears crowding to run free again. That didn’t stop Brenda, of course.

“I heard you mumbling something when you got in the car, trifecta? Please don’t tell me you’ve been betting on horses. That’s Tommy’s department.”

“Brenda, listen. No horses, no betting. I’m depressed over my own mistakes. Hormonal, I told you.”

Luckily at that point she pulled into her garage. Okay, she tried to get into the garage. Once the automatic door went up it displayed a whole assortments of boxes, furniture, even clothes, strewn all over the floor. She killed the engine while muttering about killing her nephew. I could only imagine her reaction once she saw the inside of her house. She headed to the back door and I firmly held Dior’s leash. I wanted to give Brenda enough time to assess the damages before Dior joined in and maybe got blamed for something he didn’t do.

She cussed. Loud and clear. A rare happening. Good for her. Lights came on. The brighter the lights, the louder her frustration. I followed her in; even with my cleaning there was no way of ignoring the smell of dog poop.

“Wait until I get my hands on him,” she howled as she looked at the devastation to her beautiful home. “You just wait.”

She noticed the drinking glasses on the kitchen counter, one with lipstick on the rim and instinctively turned to me. I didn't answer, couldn't answer, could only shake my head in commiseration.

"How about I help you clean up?" I offered.

I noticed an open folder on the coffee table, next to the couch where Brenda usually sat. Pages had slipped out of the folder, and I could see colorful pics of dishes and what looked like recipes. "Are you working on a cookbook?" I asked.

"Oh, that? No. Lois Thomas, Angelique's assistant, asked me to take a look to see how hard it would be to modify some of the recipes to less fat and lower calories. In other words, make them more senior-friendly."

"Interesting. So, is it hard?"

She shrugged, walked over and slid the pages back into the folder. Then, without a word she got the bottle of Pinot Grigio from the fridge. Along with clean glasses, she brought everything to the coffee table, set it next to the folder, poured some wine and nodded me over. Brenda kicked off her shoes and slumped down on the couch. After she lit a cigarette she said, "Let's drink to life without men." We did.

SIXTEEN

The call came in as I drove south on Tatum, on my way to the office. The kind of call I've dreamed of since receiving my real estate license. A prospect, a completely unknown-to me- human asked to see my brand new listing; the one with the walk-in tub. Okay, the caller never mentioned the walk-in tub, but that had become my personal, secret nickname for my adult community property. As instructed by Kay, I didn't ask the caller's age nor anything else personal, just a name and phone number — in case we got disconnected. Another clever hint from Kay. Mental note to myself, get a thank you gift for Kay and a very, very special gift for Tristan.

Aye, big mistake, just the thought of his name sent me plummeting into despair once again. *What did he share about his marriage in that message*? How could I find out? Can you retrieve deleted text messages? Who should I ask? And why? He probably will never want to talk to me again anyhow.

I drove like a distracted driver, except in my case I was my own distraction. The appointment with the caller was in ninety minutes. If I managed to stay focused, I could stop by the office, grab a cup of coffee, print out the most recent stats of the neighborhood and still get to my listing with enough time to turn on all the lights, open all the curtains, make the place look light and bright. I could hardly contain my excitement, and for an instant even my strong work ethic, as mentioned by *him*, made sense. Okay a fleeting instant. Then that went south (still trying to figure out why Americans use south instead of, you know, east, or west) as soon as I stepped into Desert Homes Realty. For one thing, Kassandra's desk was empty. I heard voices coming from the kitchen. So I headed that way. That's where the coffee was to be found anyway.

"Would you have the nerve to do that?"

Kassandra spoke with her mouth full of eggs on a muffin? Actually that looked good, I thought as I watched her stuff the last piece in her mouth.

Scott, Kassandra's audience, shrugged, picked some breadcrumbs from the corner of his mouth. "Don't know. Depends on the reason. What's there to gain?"

Neither acknowledged my presence. What? Had I become invisible?

"What are you guys talking about? And is there anything left of what you two are, or I guess have been, eating?"

"That creep who stole my bra."

Kassandra wiped her mouth first, then her hands, and tried to make a hoop into the trashcan with the scrunched up napkin; she missed.

"The cops checked out the address I gave them, you know, where we had the séance. Turned out he didn't even live there. He was housesitting for someone else. And, he was using someone else's identity to get a house-sitting job. Yeah, I think that's what the cops said. And no, no food, all gone. Scott bought some breakfast stuff from the beloved Golden Arches drive through. Well, you look perky this morning. Got your visitor?" she asked me.

My visitor? What was she talking about?

"Kassandra, Tommy was staying at Brenda's, not my place."

"Tommy? What the hell do I care where that big jerk is staying? I mean, you know."

She rubbed her hand on her belly. OMG! She asked about my period? In front of Scott? Suddenly my need for coffee evaporated. I turned on my heel and rushed over to my cubicle to look up my comps and get out of there. Noooo. Someone had shut off my computer. It takes forever to get it going. We were the only three souls in the office. Make that two souls. I grabbed my briefcase and left without saying goodbye.

Now I wasn't driving distracted, I was driving mad. Mad as hell. I couldn't believe Kassandra. What else did she tell Scott? Did she show him my test kit? *What test kit?* I never got it. The nightmare continued. Clear your mind Monica, clear your mind. Strong work ethic, remember?

Meantime, in my hurry to get away from the office, okay, from Kassandra, I didn't do my comparables. But lucky for me I had all that material J.S. had set up and left in the kitchen. Okay then, show time. I parked and got into the house. I flew from room to room getting the place ready, opening a few windows to get the stale air moving, flushing the toilets, wiping imaginary dust from the kitchen counters with some tissues I had in my purse. Found an empty plastic cup in the sink, smelled of cola and had lipstick on the rim. Did someone show the listing?

And then I waited. After a while, tired of pacing I sat on the toilet. Note to myself, bring a folding chair and leave it in the garage. Also bring a roll of paper towels because you never know when they may come in handy. My prospect was now forty-five minutes late and then it hit me. I didn't give her the gate code. How was she going to get past that? Noooo.

How could I be so careless? Strong work ethic, yeah! She could have called me? Did I miss her phone call? I checked my messages, voice mail, and texts. Nothing. What if she called my broker, told Kay what a careless agent I was? After playing all kinds of what ifs in my mind, I punched in her number. It rang four times before someone answered. "Yes?"

Didn't expect that, "Hi, it's Monica, Monica Baker, the realtor? We spoke earlier." Nothing, so I said, "You were interested on checking out my listing at..."

"Oh, yeah. Well, I forgot, I had this — thing. Can't do it today. Don't call me again, I'll call you when I'm ready."

Whaaat?

Well, I'll be. What a rude B***H. I wasted my whole morning, *like I had somewhere else to go*. So much for my first prospect. I sat on the john for a long time. Suddenly being a realtor didn't feel so good or appealing or promising. Maybe it was time to pack it up and go home.

I had money coming my way and Christmas was around the corner. I'd heard you could get last minute plane tickets cheap. And those pool pics made especially for my family, I could deliver them in person. Images of myself dressed as Santa Claus,

Babbo Natale, bringing gifts from America, flashed through my mind and made me feel oh, so weepy. Screw this!

I flushed the toilet in a gesture of defiance, went around to close the house and found a note by the stack of fliers. From the sellers. "*Great job Monica, we come by from time to time, hope you don't mind.*" Oh, that explained the stain in the sink, I sighed. Good. One less worry. All good. Twenty minutes later I was on my way back to the Desert Homes Real Estate office. But the taste of the breakfast food had been lingering somewhere between my brain and my stomach, so when I spotted the yellow arches, a quick sharp turn got me there. Breakfast in the afternoon. Only in America. God, I love this country!

By the time I parked my Fiat, I counted five cars in the office parking lot. Okay, one was Kassandra's Kia. Scott's truck wasn't there. Sonny's Cadillac occupied her assigned spot but I didn't recognized the two black, imposing sedans. Not like money imposing, more like 'official something' imposing. I checked my lips and teeth in the side mirror. The last thing I needed was left over egg yolk on my teeth; I fluffed my hair and tried to walk as professionally as possible. I have no idea how a professional real estate agent of the female persuasion walks, but one could give her own spin. On that thought, I almost got knocked to the ground by someone opening the office door on me.

"Sorry miss," he mumbled. He looked vaguely familiar. Ah, a cop. Not officer Clarke, him I would know for sure. I dawdled before going in and watched the plain clothes cop go to one of the black sedans, open the front passenger door and search for something in the glove compartment and front seat. When he slammed the door shut I quickly let myself into the lobby and closed the door behind me. Didn't want Mister Cop to think I was snooping. After all, that's his job.

A sense of excitement hovered over the office.

Kassandra's welcoming, "There you are," bolstered my spirits and then the cop came back from the parking lot and stopped by Kassandra's desk.

I could see Sunny standing by her office door, talking to... oh no, the two detectives, Adam and Eve I called them. The ones investigating the death of Miss Fortune. Somehow the excitement in the air took a dark turn as a little voice kept repeating, investigating the *murder* of Miss Fortune. I was done trying to eavesdrop, and without a word, I headed toward my cubicle. Obviously not fast enough because Sunny called out to and waved me over.

What now? This day was growing weirder by the minute. I could see a young woman in the back of the bullpen; she must be new, and shy from what I could see of the top of her head as she bent low in front of her computer. That explained the fifth vehicle in the parking lot. I should go say hi, make her feel at ease.

"Monica." Sunny's voice changed my mind and I headed her way.

Kassandra and the other cop were right behind me, headed in the same direction. What was going on? We all stood by my old desk, in front of Sunny's glass office. And to say I felt a little uncomfortable was like saying Godzilla was a little monkey.

"Monica, the detectives are here to show us some photos of the person or persons who may have — hurt — the uh, psychic. What I mean is, they are here to show the photos to Kassandra and..." She paused, cleared her throat. "Kassandra and Celine, to see if they remember or recognize or..."

Her eyes traveled back and forth from the front door to the desk, and then I got it. Celine was a no show. Poor Sunny, trying to keep the charade going until her daughter arrived.

"Anyway, I was wondering if you would mind taking Kassandra's place for about fifteen minutes, while..."

"Yes... sure, absolutely," I said in a gentle tone. Couldn't wait to get the hell away from that crowded group. Just then the door cop dropped a folder on my old desk too close to the edge and it slid right off, landing on the floor. A few large black and white photos fell out. Both Kassandra and I bent to help pick them up.

The strangest thing happened. We accidentally picked up the same photo, "Shit, that's him," Kassandra cried out.

"Oh, I know him," I said. "That's the guy who chased me the other day." We were both looking at the same face: the face of J.S.'s dad.

After that there was no way Sunny was going to send me to mind the front desk. The three detectives were more excited than three blind mice sitting on top of a wheel of *Parmigiano Reggiano*. Of course I had to tell the whole story about my borrowing Kassandra's Kia and my not so good driving habits. Well, that didn't go over well with Kassandra, who wanted to know why I didn't tell her. Duh! Seems pretty self-explanatory judging by the way she looked at me. I could swear at some point she foamed a little at the mouth.

It quickly became apparent that the man in the photo followed the Kia, not the driver; he was trying to find Kassandra.

"I may have saved your life," I proclaimed. All I got was an eye roll. What an ingrate friend. So J.S.'s dad was the perp who hosted the séance, attacked Kassandra, and probably stole the money collected to pay for the psychic. At that point I related how the man was trying to steal from the R.E. Assist's van and his daughter caught him.

"Do you know where this J.S. lives?" Detective Eve asked me.

"No idea, but she works for R.E Assist as a photographer, and a very good one at that."

Sunny moved her hand by her lips to tell me to zip it. My mouth, she meant. So I did.

Meanwhile, Detective Adam was already on the phone with R.E. Assist, but got a recording. He didn't look too happy. That's when, in spite of Sunny's warning. I shouted, "By George, I think I've got it."

When all heads turned my way I explained, "*My Fair Lady*... the scene..."

If looks could kill, I would have died a quick and lasting death thanks to the five pair of eyes.

"Sorry." I toned it down a notch. "I like old movies. But I meant, Kassandra said the man from the séance went by Bill Smith? Well J.S.'s last name is Smith, so you see, she may well have been telling the truth."

More eye rolls and heads shaking. No one took me seriously, too concerned about Kassandra.

Detective Adam furrowed his brow and said, “It’s obvious the man is after you, so you must know something. We need to have someone keep you safe 24/7.”

Detectives Adam and Eve exchanged glances. Then Eve said, “We’ll follow you home. Park in your usual spot and we’ll have surveillance set up.”

“Does she get to pick?” I asked.

“Pick? Pick what Miss Baker?” Detective Eve mocked me.

“Not what, whom? The officer spending time with her I mean.”

“Oh, brother,” Kassandra puffed and turned her back on me. How rude.

“No, Miss Baker the surveillance is done from an unmarked car.”

Apparently no one was concerned about my well being, because everyone was busy talking a mile a minute to Kassandra and Sunny. Why Sunny? She didn’t even go to the fair. Well, neither did I. After a bit, I picked up my stuff, sneaked out of the office and headed home.

SEVENTEEN

Bite the bullet, Monica, bite the bullet. I had been sitting in my parked car, watching the entrance to the Walgreen's closest to my house for the last fifteen minutes. Waiting for my Catholic upbringing to give me a break so I could buy the pregnancy test kit and find out just how much trouble I was in. How hard could it be? Go in, grab the kit from the shelf, go to the cashier, pay cash, and voilà. Untraceable. Untraceable? Seriously, I was losing it. Like buying a pregnancy test was illegal or something. I was well over twenty-one, in case there was an age restriction. I could always say it was for a friend. *Who's going to ask?* Besides, if I kept sitting there and staring at the entrance someone was bound to assume I was casing the joint. Oh, to steal a pregnancy test kit? Sheeesh.

I got out of the car and walked to the drug store with the same ease as Sean Penn's last stroll in the movie *Dead Man Walking*. I could use Susan Sarandon's words of encouragement.

A side glance to the cashier's counter – an unknown older woman. Perfect. I kept on moving trying to read the signs describing the products on the aisles. Ah, there it was. Feminine products. Few people in the store. A man in the greeting cards aisle; a young woman looking at garden products. I quickened my pace, turned to Aisle 5… and bumped into the forever over-perfumed widow from across the street. NO!

"Oh, hi Monica, I think I'm confused. I'm looking for shampoo. This one." She flashed a discount coupon under my nose.

"Aw, shucks. Can you believe it? So am I, but I forgot my coupon. Anyway, I think it's on the next aisle, under Hair Products. Well, better run home and get my coupon. See you."

And like the coward I am, I rushed past the distracted cashier, back to my car and home.

My mood improved when I realized Brenda was home alone. I didn't take the time to run by my place to change, I let myself in through the back door so quickly I even surprised Dior. That was a first.

"Someone has been busy," I declared loudly, making Brenda jump. She, who always relied on her dog's alerts, reacted quickly, and not in a good way. I mean, the Dane was sleeping on the job. *Bad doggie.* And look at that. Someone cleaned the house. I could clearly see the floors. Hmmm. What happened to the home gym project?

"Hey, Monica, come here."

Brenda walked to her pantry to die for. The place where her famous catered parties always came to life first. On paper I mean. It was like a ritual. Brenda standing at the center of her pantry, backed by her five corkboards, channeling her inner — chef? Nah, it was a lot more than that. She had a talent for taking the tritest of recipes and turning them into delicious new culinary creations. Often with the same ingredients. In part thanks to her Registered Dietitian background and the rest thanks to her genuine love of nutrition, food, or whatever you want to call it.

"Brenda, last evening your place looked like a disaster area. And now, it's like a miracle."

"Yeah, a $150 miracle. I hired some of the busboys from work and decided I would be better off with my treadmill and weights in my bedroom instead of messing with the perfect pantry."

I nodded. "Wise investment. Hey, did you lose weight?"

"Hmmm, only two pounds. But it's a start. By the way, I'm working on Kay's Christmas party. It's going to be a sit down affair, very elegant. I stopped by her place on my way home. Do you know she lives in one of the top floors of that tall building at the corner of Camelback and 24th street? The place is over 2,000 square feet with breathtaking views from every window. Unfortunately, the kitchen is a galley type, too inconvenient for us to do all the cooking there. I already spoke to Leta, my trusted, wonderful right-hand assistant, and we'll do the main cooking here and finish up the details at Kay's. Oh, and Leta says hi."

"Thanks, I love Leta, too. But what's a galley kitchen? Sounds awful."

Brenda laughed, that raspy laugh I had missed so much. "A *galley kitchen* is a narrow space, characterized by two parallel countertops that incorporate a walking area in between. So while it's a good layout under normal circumstances, it won't do when you have several people working together. Especially cooks with wide hips," she added, in self-mocking mode.

"Anyway, Kay is pretty set on the menu, which is a blessing and a curse. As we know, not all taste buds perform the same way."

"Are you cooking something?" An interesting smell wafted from the kitchen.

"You just now noticed? What's wrong with your nose? Do you have a cold?" Brenda chided me.

"What's cooking, what's cooking?" Dior's ears perked up for an instant, then he went back to sleep. Must not be anything involving meat or he'd be sleeping sprawled in front of the stove.

"I'm trying out fat-free recipes, per Angelique Dumont's request."

Puff went my happy evening. No matter how hard I tried, I kept bumping into some Dumont-related news. *Maledizione*. At least we managed to avoid the Tommy subject.

"Tell me more, tell me more," I hummed.

"I'm trying out a banana bread made with gluten free flour and apple sauce instead of oil. I'm also baking boneless pork chops brushed with mustard and mayonnaise as a substitute for oil and salt. That's a brand new concoction I came up with. We'll see. You're welcome to stay and try out the results."

"I thought you'd never ask," I said, kicking off my shoes and heading for the couch, with a little detour to the refrigerator where the Pinot Grigio always waited patiently. Meanwhile, my mind churned away at all the news, good or bad, I should probably share with Brenda, especially about the man who may have killed Miss Fortune. Wait, her buddy officer Clarke had probably already told her all about it. What if he hadn't? *Proceed with caution*?

"Hey Brenda, how is your friend, Bob?" There, that was neutral enough,

"Let me finish my notes for Kay's party before I forget."

"OK." The oven bell went off.

"Perfect timing," Brenda announced from the pantry. I didn't move. It suddenly dawned on me that in spite of all the detectives' good will, how could they be sure Smith, the creep, was after Kassandra? He followed me once when I drove the Kia. However, our second encounter at my listing, I was driving... nothing. J.S. had given me a ride in her van. Whoa! Big sigh of relief.

"What was that all about?"

I hadn't seen Brenda coming from the kitchen, oven mittens on, showing me the wonderful golden crusty top of the banana bread hot from the stove. The smell alone had me drooling.

"We can have a slice for dessert. How about a pork chop and a salad first?"

"Yes, yes, yes." *Do I tell her about Mr. Smith or do I keep my mouth shut?*

This felt like casual night. We ate in the living room. I sat on the floor, my plate on the low coffee table and Dior slouching by my feet, looking at me with hungry eyes. What an actor.

"How is Officer Clarke?" I asked again between bites.

She stopped eating, fork in midair and turned to look at me square in the eyes, "Young lady, let's get this out of the way once for all. Bob is a good friend. We are both single, never married. He knows my story, spent hours cheering me up and sharing his own troubles. He lives with his elderly mother who suffers from dementia. While we are good friend there is *nothing* romantic between us. Got it? Can we move past this?"

I found myself gulping air. Dior must have assumed I lost my appetite because he swiftly grabbed the last bite of meat left on my plate and rushed toward the kitchen. Brenda and I had to hide our surprised grins. She did say something to him, but by then he was probably hiding under the kitchen table, licking his chops. Bandit.

That was my cue to tell Brenda about the detectives' visit to the office, the photo of the perp and Kassandra's and my unplanned contribution to solving the identity of the mysterious man walking away from the Psychic Fair with Miss Fortune. In retrospect, my shared news killed the mood. The rest of the evening was spent with Brenda worrying about me and offering her guest room for the night. Let's see, do I take a chance on Mr. Smith finding his way into my own bedroom or do I spend the night at Brenda's hoping my ex doesn't find his way back and into the guest room? The choice came easy. I walked home with two slices of banana bread in a sandwich bag.

I had barely changed into my pajamas when my cell chimed. My heart skipped a beat as the name Tristan lit up the corner of my heart where hope flourished. Not for long, as it was only Kassandra calling.

"Once again, I didn't get you the pregnancy kit. How pissed at me are you? Oh, and before you answer, be aware that the good guys may be listening to our conversation. They are bugging my phone in case that creep calls." Needless to say, I felt... speechless.

"Is that why you called? To tell me about the cops listening in?"

"Oh, no, no. I've been doing my Tarot cards for you and this is rather strange. I keep coming up with the wheel of fortune. Maybe you'll sell that new listing yourself or maybe something unexpected is coming your way. I'm going to sleep on this and do it again in the morning. I was hoping to have an answer regarding, you know, being late but it's not telling me a thing."

What got into her? Calling me late in the evening to tell me basically nothing? "Kassandra, are you scared?"

"Scared? Why should I be scared? There's a cop watching my place. And really, I can take that sick fool. The detective told me that Miss Fortune was dead before she hit the water. Something about head trauma. The bra around the neck was more for show than anything else. Shit, why are we talking about this stuff anyhow? Okay, see you at the office in the morning. I'll bring the test kit. Going to take a bubble bath. Night. "

I hated myself for mentioning being scared to Kassandra. It sounded like I was more concerned about her than she was about herself. Well, she was a risk taker. Buying pregnancy test kits by the dozen? Wasn't she practicing safe sex? Shoot, I did and look at me. I may be pregnant. Damn.

EIGHTEEN

Holiday season or not, I had to accelerate my efforts to drum up business. With January around the corner, all the yearly fees and dues had to be paid, and that accounted for a nice chunk of money. Plus, because of Brenda's incident, we hadn't done much catering. Not much? My last paid gig was the Dumont's fall party. Way back before Thanksgiving. The little voice inside my head kept reminding me about the $10,000 settlement coming soon to a bank near my checking account. Let's see, I could use the money due from Tristan for his wrecked car and his injuries to pay my real estate dues? That was wrong in so many ways.

I brushed my teeth and glanced at myself in the mirror. Yuck. Thank God I had a haircut appointment today at eleven-thirty. And once again, nothing else for the rest of the day. Unless I wanted to go take up room at the office. I missed the busy days, the chatty bullpen where we gathered mostly to gossip when no clients were around. With nothing important to do, today would be a good day to go gift shopping for Kay and Tristan.

Kassandra called from the office around ten, just to announce that my luck with Tarot cards had not improved. She also mentioned that she didn't know if the cops had the office under surveillance or if it was only something they did at night, at her place. But more important, the detectives were still trying to locate J.S. Smith to see if she could help them find her father.

"What do you mean they can't locate her? They can't find her? Surely her boss knows where she's taking pics. The company supplies all the leads."

"True that. Supposedly, she didn't have any appointments the rest of the week, mainly due to the season. Therefore, she took three days off and headed out of town. Having been with this company only a few weeks and working by appointment only, no one knows much about her and no one answers the door at her place."

"She has a cell phone; is anyone calling her?"

"Why are you asking me? I don't think I've ever met her. Have I?"

"I bet Tristan Dumont would know where she hangs out," I said. "They went to the same college. They may even have shared some extracurricular activities, not sure."

"Listen to you. For someone who runs the other way when you see dream boy approach, you sure know a lot about him."

I kept quiet. Kassandra had a point. How did I end up collecting all that info about this man? More important, what did he know about me? He knew about my pierced navel... said the devilish voice in my head.

Lisa's hair studio, a one-person affair, sat smack in the center of Scottsdale's night scene. But considering she closed shop at four pm, it didn't matter to her and it didn't matter to me. Plus, it made for easy parking until the sun went down and dozens of night spots lit up.

I was back in my car and driving off way before two pm. She cut my hair a bit shorter than usual because it grew so fast. It still brushed my shoulders and I could wear it in a ponytail if necessary. I left Scottsdale behind and headed toward Paradise Valley Mall with specific shopping ideas in mind. Kay was an easy task. *Things Remembered,* tucked away in a forgotten mall corner thanks to the Costco addition, was my go-to place for anything personalized. I ordered a crystal and silver name plaque for her desk. It also said, Realtor and Mentor Extraordinaire. The idea was to have Brenda or Leta sneak the wrapped gift under Kay's Christmas tree the night of the catered affair. An affair to which apparently no co-workers were invited. And that included me. Tristan's, on the other hand, was a bit more complicated and still a work in progress. I turned the corner, planning on cutting through the food court to get back to the covered parking. My eyes were drawn to the brightly decorated windows and I nearly bumped into of all people, Lois Thomas gingerly pushing a wheel chair with a relaxed and contented-looking Angelique Dumont. You could have knocked me over with a sparrow feather.

I tried to play dumb, but Angelique called out to me. "Monica, what a pleasant surprise."

And with that kind hello, I was trapped. Inside I squirmed like a gold fish flipped out of its tank, but I had my best smile on and a freshly cut head of hair. Bring it on.

After a few minutes of my changing foot dance, we ended up on the top level where the seating accommodations were cushy and didn't include food. It turned out the two women were also gift shopping and the wheel chair was one of those light folding things people keep in the trunk of the car. Apparently, as Lois pointed out, Angelique's health had been improving by leaps and bounds, probably due to Arizona's favorable climate and easy access to attentive medical personnel. I felt as at ease as a Buckingham Palace Guard with poison ivy in his skivvies. Merci me. The two women had nothing but kind things to say about Brenda and me.

Just when I thought it couldn't get any more awkward, Angelique said, "Why don't you come visit us when Tristan is back from his trip? And bring your dog, the Great Dane. Tristan can't stop talking about the way his Tache and your dog like each other."

On my way to find the car, all I could think about was how badly I needed a drink or a shrink. So instead of heading home, I made a U-turn and took the road to the Desert Homes Real Estate office. Not sure why. Everyone had gone to an afternoon affair put on by the Scottsdale Association of Realtors, to which I might add, we all paid dues. But I chose to skip it and Kassandra wasn't invited since she was a civilian. I always got her riled up when I said that. Well today was her lucky day. I would pay for happy hour in exchange for the pregnancy test kit she had sworn to bring to the office.

It was after four by the time I drove into the parking lot where the Kia sat in all her loneliness. My cell chimed. It was an agent from Homesmart requesting permission to show my walk-in tub listing in the morning. Yesssss!

If I could just get a negative on the test, I'd be the happiest girl on earth. Well, sort of. I kept wondering where Tristan was. Angelique mentioned a trip. Maybe he went to Vegas to get a divorce? Stop it, Monica. Besides, he may never speak to you again. I didn't even lock my car. I figured I'd be out of the office and on my way to happy hour in a jiffy. That is, until I got to the front door of Desert Homes Real Estate and found it locked. What the h**l?

What was Kassandra up to now? Would she be so brazen as to have a man in there? Nah. I never knew her to be anything but professional at work. Okay, except for that time when she showed up braless. Not exactly the image I needed in my head; poor Miss Fortune. Why would J.S.'s dad kill her? Wait, no one called him the killer yet. He was 'a person of interest.'

I tried the door again. There wasn't a door bell to ring so I knocked. It would take a baseball bat to knock loud enough. The door was massive. So I dialed Kassandra's cell first and when the call went directly to voice mail, I tried the office number with the same results.

The sudden stiffening of the hair on the back of my neck wasn't exactly the result of an early evening breeze. I slowly backed away and returned to my car. Maybe Kassandra was in the bathroom. Or maybe she stepped out to run an errand. On foot? And why wasn't she answering her phone? Where was her surveillance? Breathe, Monica, breathe.

There was a card that allowed agents to open the door after hours, except I never asked for mine. Damn. I could have slid the thing in and voilà, open sesame.

I needed to clear my head and try Kassandra's phone again. I started the engine and went around the block, paying close attention to parked cars, looking for trucks and campers. Any clue. Nothing looked familiar and my phone calls all ended up in voicemail. When I returned to the parking lot, the outside lights of the building were lit, but they were set to come on at dusk automatically. No lights at all inside. I sat there, like a pile of laundry waiting to be sorted. When my cell chimed I jumped.

"Hey," Brenda said.

I sighed. "Brenda, something weird is going on." Then I spilled the beans, leaving out the part about the pregnancy kit.

"Monica, listen and listen good. Get yourself out of there now. Promise me. I'm calling somebody, but you need to get out of there. Okay?"

"OK." I said, fingers crossed as I just lied to her. I had an idea. As soon as she hung up I got out of my car and walked over to the Kia. *Please, please god, let the car to be unlocked.* It must have been a light work day in heaven because Kassandra's car wasn't locked. I prayed some more, in case she had some silent alarm or something. Then again, this was Kassandra's car. No alarm. I rummaged through her console, the glove compartment and then I checked behind her sun visor. Bingo. Although I'd never really handled one of those magnetic cards, something told me that was the one. I got out of the Kia, closed the door quietly and walked over to the front door of the office to Desert Homes.

I heard a click. It worked. The door was now unlocked. My hand on the handle shook. Not a sound came from inside. The shaking spread, from my hands, through my body, to my legs. Must do this. Now. The beat of my heart would awake even Sleeping Beauty on horse tranquillizers. Must do this. I pushed the door open.

NINETEEN

I closed the front door slowly, trying to avoid making noises. I couldn't see or hear a thing. As my eyes became accustomed to the quickly disappearing daylight, I noticed things. Like Kassandra's desk, without Kassandra. I moved closer. So tense, I worried about stumbling and falling. The first oddity was Kassandra's chair, sideways on the floor, next to her desk. The sweater she kept draped on the back of the chair still partly hooked on it, but dragging on the floor. That was the only visible proof of Kassandra's presence.

The purse kept under the desk? Gone.

I tiptoed around, looking for her personal cell: missing. However, the office phone had an orangey light, blinking. I kept tiptoeing toward the back of the room, too frightened to check the kitchen because it only had one way in and out.

Oddly, I remembered some of the cop shows pointing out how you should always have an alternate escape route. Just in case.

I skipped the kitchen.

The whole time I thought, whoever didn't belong here was probably watching my every move. Maybe I should be brave and call out Kassandra's name. But being brave didn't feel like a smart thing to do.

Then I stepped on something that didn't belong on the floor. Broken glass, and not like a lens from reading glasses. Nope, a sea of shards. I held on tight to my cell phone, as if it would save me should someone jump out of nowhere. I kept moving carefully, but there was no way I could avoid all the broken glass. Where did it come from?

Wait, what if someone called me. On the phone. No, no. Can't happen. That would certainly give me away. I fumbled to put my cell on vibrate. Not easy with sweaty palms and shaky hands. I crunched glass at every step, bypassed my cubicle, the bullpen, and saw it. Someone had thrown my old chair through the glass door of Sunny's office. That whole front wall of glass had come tumbling down. The inside of the office looked like a bomb had exploded. Fading light from the large window cast dancing shadows on the papers and files dotting the floor. Even the drawers had been pulled out and dumped in disarray. The only sign of life, just as at the front desk, was the blinking light on Sunny's desk phone.

I turned to peek outside the only window. It opened onto the parking lot, and I could clearly see my pink Fiat sitting under the street light. Maybe that was my cue. Get the hell out of there and call 911. I quickened my pace. Hey, I was no hero, and for all I knew Kassandra might have left with a friend way before some creep, high on illegal stuff, broke in here. If only we had a security system.

There was one more place I neglected to check. Kay's office. *Only one way in and out*, the little voice in my head whispered. True, but no need to go *into* the closet-size office; all I had to do was open the door and stick my head in. I veered that way. Obviously, whoever the vandal or vandals were, they had also walked this way. More than one of the bullpen computers rested scattered on the floor. I paused. Kay's door only feet from me. *Do the right thing*. Why? "You know why," my grandmother's voice proclaimed from the grave.

Screw this. Two steps and my right hand reached out in defiance and twisted the doorknob with all my might. And – it came lose, fell out of my hand and hit the floor with a thud that sounded to me like a volcano eruption. Obviously, someone had already made it into Kay's office.

I turned around and took off running – forget tiptoeing and the silent treatment. I had to get out of there. I felt my cell vibrate in my hand – a call coming in. I slowed for a nanosecond to swipe the screen. I could hear a faint voice calling my name just as a large shadow came rushing at me from the kitchen. It came to a stop, then bolted to intercept my exit. I felt trapped, but kept moving. Now the man, as I had no doubt it was a man, stood squarely between me and the front door. And he looked familiar. In a threateningly familiar way. So much for an alternate escape route.

Bill Smith, J.S.'s estranged father, stood looking at me looking at him. Damn. There we were, both panting, adrenaline rushing. Assessing our chances? Funny Monica, real funny. He moved a little to take command of the whole doorframe. Then the phone on Kassandra's desk rang and I almost jumped out of my skin. Meanwhile, the monologue on my cell continued. I had no clue who had called me except that the voice was male. I faked a sudden move toward the desk and Bill Smith fell for it. He leaped in that direction and I rushed toward the front door.

Didn't make it. He grabbed my hair and yanked so hard, I fell backward, still holding my cell as a lifebuoy. I hit the hard floor and the room began to spin. I heard a crash coming from somewhere. The kitchen? Just then his boot hit my right ribs. I screamed, rolling on the floor anticipating his next kick when suddenly the lights came on.

Someone had opened the front door. Everything changed. Flashing lights. Police sirens? Help must have arrived, I told myself. My phone had gone quiet. So did I. I closed my eyes, the aching from my body so intense I couldn't breathe and hundreds of stabbing, throbbing pains were shooting into my legs. Things came in waves. The scuffle next to me, someone apprehending Smith, EMTs rushing in and out. Pushing a gurney? No, please, not Kassandra. I wanted to yell, but no sound came, only warm tears washing over my cheeks. Where was she? In the kitchen? I should have gone in there; it was my fault.

Someone was talking to me, in person talking to me, not on my phone. Where was my phone? Ouch, ouch. Hands lifted me off the floor and laid me on something soft. Was I dying? I couldn't be, I had things to do. Christmas cards to send to Mom. People to say goodbye to... slowly nothing mattered and darkness and silence lulled me away.

"Look at this as your glory day," Brenda, in all her fond sarcasm, declared. I sat in the hospital bed, my back propped up by so many pillows, I figured one wrong move and I'd suffocate in all that fluffiness. Visitors had been coming and going. Sunny, weepy because she felt partly responsible due to the lack of a security system. Kay, telling me not to worry about my real estate deals because she had my back. Officer Clarke? Oh, Bob to his friends was there, too, proud as a peacock because he was the voice on my phone who, according to his version of the facts, guided me to the front door and to salvation. The one I really wanted to see, didn't come around.

Eventually I was ready to go home, but first I insisted on Brenda taking me to see Kassandra. I learned she was in the same hospital, but on a different floor, in ICU. Everyone assured me she would pull through with flying colors, and it was only a matter of a day or so and she would be moved to a regular ward. Still, I had to see her with my own eyes.

The afternoon of my release I wore clean clothes Brenda brought from home. A dozen band aids dotted my arms and legs where I'd cut myself on the broken glass while rolling on the floor. Brenda and Bob piloted my wheel chair, per hospital rules, to Kassandra's room.

The ICU floor seemed so much quieter, all hushed voices, closed doors. Kassandra, the fearless, badass girl, looked so small and defenseless in the hospital bed. The room smelled of sanitizers and cough medicine. The bandages covered her whole head, including her cinnamon mane, and framed her swollen, bruised face. What had Smith done to her? She must have put up a hell of a fight. I couldn't see her body, but tubes, probably IVs, were visible. And so were Kassandra's hands. Skinned knuckles and all.

In all that misery, her eyes burned bright. I sensed that Kassandra wanted to talk, but probably couldn't. Using my feet I pushed the wheel chair as close to the bed as possible and then placed my ear up to Kassandra's lips.

"Thank you."

More hiss than words, but what else is needed between best friends? I patted Kassandra's hand lightly, then bent close to her face again and whispered, "Hey, I owe you one. In all that excitement I got my period."

A little hiccup under the blankets told me Kassandra was trying to laugh.

We drove home in Brenda's Honda. Bob had brought my Fiat back to the house that very morning. "Does anyone know what this creep wanted from Kassandra?" I asked.

"The investigation is still ongoing." Bob spoke as if the future of the world hinged on his words. Mercy.

"This is crazy. Are we sure he killed Miss Fortune? What for?" It dawned on me no one even mentioned his daughter, J.S. Ah!

Brenda was driving and I could see her looking at me in the rear view mirror. "He claims it was all a misunderstanding, an accident."

"Seriously, Brenda? That's his defense? Good luck with that." My voice was shaking with anger. I ran my hands over the stiff bandages covering my torso, hidden by my sweater. "I hope he rots in jail."

Neither answered me. I sat quietly for the rest of the ride and, once home, I made it clear I was sleeping in my own bed. No babysitting needed, thank you very much. To my surprise no one objected. After Bob helped me out of the SUV and Brenda handed me my belongings the hospital nurses had packed, they watched me walk into my place and slam the door shut. How is that for gratitude? It didn't ease my conscience finding the refrigerator stocked with food and drinks, fresh linens on the bed and in the bath, and my cell sitting on the charger. Still, I stewed. Why?

My anger left me as quickly as it found me. Fatigue settled in. I lined up the few medications I'd been instructed to take. Then I sat on the bed and turned on the television.

One of the local channels had a special report on Bill Smith and the dead psychic. Seriously? Can't a girl catch a break? But instead of changing channels I turned up the volume.

The TV reporter stood in front of a construction site. Hmmm, Miss Fortune was found floating in the canal. I heard her say, "The old apartment building was demolished months ago to make room for a new condo complex..." and a light bulb went off over my poor, aching head.

OMG! That must be Kassandra's old address, the one she never changed with the Department of Motor Vehicles. Now I paid attention.

Miss Fortune had planned on spending the night at Kassandra's place, except Kassandra was a no show at the séance. Enter Bill Smith, by then homeless and living in the camper. He offered to drive the psychic to Kassandra's home, he said. In reality he intended to rob both women. Miss Fortune tried to call Kassandra, but had no luck. And since she didn't know Kassandra had moved, she gave Smith the address listed on the séance roster. Smith claimed that by the time they arrived at the Scottsdale site and realized there was no Kassandra, he got upset and argued with Miss Fortune. She stumbled and fell, hitting her head.

After loading the body into his camper, he drove west on Indian School Road and got the idea of discarding the dead woman in the canal that runs along the street. He had Kassandra's bra in the camper and tightened it around Miss Fortune's neck in hopes the authorities would suspect Kassandra. Well, he got that right. But why hurt Kassandra?

Apparently, Smith had kept Miss Fortune's phone. The detectives found it and discovered several calls she'd made to Kassandra. Two of them were after she had accepted the ride from Smith. He had no idea Miss Fortune never reached Kassandra. Instead, he must have thought she would be the only one who could rat him out, telling the detectives that the victim had been in his truck when she called.

I could only imagine how giddy he felt when he spotted Kassandra's Kia, only to find me in the driver's seat. It wasn't hard for him to figure out that we worked together. He put two and two together after our second unfortunate encounter, when he ran into J.S. and her van from R.E. Assist, and saw me with the For Sale sign with Desert Homes Real Estate. I wondered how long he had been casing the office to find Kassandra alone at closing time.

Enough sadness for one day. I turned off the television, got some water and my evening pill. My phone chimed. Yes, it was back to life, back to business, sort of.

"Hello." No answer, I didn't recognize the number. "Who the hell is this?" My frustration was back as if it had never left me.

"Fiat," he said, followed by a soft chuckle. "I was about to ask how you feel. But I can tell you're in top form."

Tristan? Be still my heart.

"I… I… am okay." Breathe Monica, breathe. "You're not mad at me?"

Long pause. "How can I be mad at you? I'm gone for two days and you make the news. Tried calling your cell." He paused.

It was coming back to me now, why I was so angry. Because the most important person in my life didn't visit me at the hospital. "Where are you?"

"Airport, waiting to board my flight home. I'm glad to know you're okay. Maybe I'll see you when I get back?"

"Okay, yes. Yes." I hung up. Why? Because he was still a married man. And I was scared, of my own feelings. Perhaps Brenda was right. It was time for me to ask the questions if I wanted to know the answers.

As soon as he returned to town and I could safely drive myself around. Like Scarlett O'Hara said, "After all, tomorrow is another day."

I stretched out on the bed, rested my head on the pillow. My eyelids felt heavy; must be the pill.

I dreamed of Tristan and his Appaloosa, riding into the sunset.

~~~~~~~~~~~~
~~~~~~~~~~~~

LOW FAT BANANA BREAD

Heat oven to 350 degrees F
Coat a 9"x5"x3"baking pan with a light coat of non-stick cooking spray

1 ¾ cups of unbleached all purpose flour
2 teaspoons double acting baking powder
¼ teaspoon baking soda
½ teaspoon salt
1/2 cup unsweetened applesauce
2/3 cup granulated sugar
2 whole eggs, beaten
1 cup mashed ripe bananas, approximately 2-3 medium

Sift flour, baking powder, soda and salt together and set aside.

With an electric mixer on medium speed mix applesauce and sugar until well blended, and then add eggs until mixture is light and fluffy.

With the electric mixer at low speed or by hand to be sure you don't over beat, fold in flour mixture, alternating with mashed bananas until smooth.

Pour into prepared baking pan. Bake 1 hour or until cake tester inserted in center comes out clean. Do not overbake. You can cool for 10 minutes and remove from pan or you can let it cool an hour and slice directly from the pan.

FOR GLUTEN FREE RECIPE

If you want a gluten free recipe you can substitute the regular flour with gluten free flour and if you want to avoid binders, bake banana muffins instead of banana bread. Makes one dozen muffins. Use baking cups to avoid using grease for the muffin pan.

Bake muffins at 400 degrees for 25 minutes or until done.

MONICA'S 3 MINUTE NO-BAKE DESSERT

Frozen organic silver dollar pancakes
Nutella
Canned whipped cream

Place 2 silver dollar pancakes on a microwave safe dish. Approximately 25 calories per pancake.

Microwave for 15 seconds or until just warm.

Spread 1/3 teaspoon Nutella (approximately 25 calories) on each pancake with butter knife, squeeze a tablespoon whipped cream on each pancake (approximately 15 calories).

Total calories for each complete pancake is about 65 calories. And it's good for you… Enjoy.

Free Italian recipe for Hot Chocolate

Sign up for my occasional newsletter to be the first to know about new releases, deals and giveaways. As a thank you I will email you a link to this old family recipe for hot chocolate. *Mille Grazie*

http://mariagraziaswan.com/sign-up-for-my-occasional-newsletter/

BOOKS BY MARIA GRAZIA SWAN

Baker Girls Cozy Mystery Series

Food, Fools and a Dead Psychic #1

Cooks, Crooks and a Corpse #2

Wine, Dine and Christmas Crimes #3

Lella York Series

Gemini Moon #1

Venetain Moon #2

Desert Moon #3

Mina's Adventure Series

Love Thy Sister #1

Bosom Bodies #2

Italian Summer #3

Ashes of Autumn #4

A Cat to Die For #5

Best in Show #6

Sniffing Out Murder #7

About the Author

Award-winning author Maria Grazia Swan was born in Italy. She's lived in Belgium, France, Germany, Southern California and Arizona – all juicy places that fuel her stories and characters. She won her first literary award, in Belgium, when she was fourteen. As a young woman Maria Grazia designed haute couture clothes in Italy, and then she took the leap and moved to America where she raised her family.

These days, Maria Grazia volunteers at the animal shelter seeking the perfect family for homeless pets. Her deepest passions? Writing and being the matchmaker for people and pets who are waiting to find each other.

Maria loves travel, opera, good books, hiking, and intelligent movies. Her idea of a perfect evening? Stimulating conversation, Northern Italian food, and chilled Prosecco.

She loves to hear from her readers! Feel free to contact her through her website:
www.mariagraziaswan.com

www.ingramcontent.com/pod-product-compliance
Ingram Content Group UK Ltd.
Pitfield, Milton Keynes, MK11 3LW, UK
UKHW021931200726
13853UKWH00010B/155

9 798201 333812